BRONSHTEIN IN THE BRONX

Books by Robert Littell

Fiction

The Defection of A.J.Lewinter

Sweet Reason

The October Circle

Mother Russia

The Debriefing

The Amateur

The Sisters

The Once and Future Spy

An Agent in Place

The Visiting Professor

Walking Back the Cat

The Revolutionist

The Company

Legends

Vicious Circle

The Stalin Epigram

Young Philby

A Nasty Piece of Work

The Mayakovsky Tapes

Comrade Koba

A Plague on Both Your Houses

Bronshtein in the Bronx

Nonfiction

For the Future of Israel (with co-author Shimon Peres)

BRONSHTEIN IN THE BRONX

ROBERT LITTELL

SOHO

Published by
Soho Press, Inc.
227 W 17th Street
New York, NY 10011

This is a work of fiction. Names, characters, places, and incidents either are the product of the author's imagination or are used fictitiously.

Library of Congress Cataloging-in-Publication Data
Names: Littell, Robert, 1935- author.
Title: Bronshtein in the Bronx / Robert Littell.
Description: New York, NY : Soho, 2025.
Identifiers: LCCN 2024030865 |

ISBN 978-1-64129-686-1
eISBN 978-1-64129-687-8

Subjects: LCSH: Trotsky, Leon, 1879-1940—Fiction. | New York—Fiction.
LCGFT: Novels.
Classification: LCC PS3562.I7827 B76 2025
DDC 813'.54—dc23/eng/20240705
LC record available at https://lccn.loc.gov/2024030865

Interior design by Janine Agro

Printed in the United States of America

10 9 8 7 6 5 4 3 2 1

For my brother, Alan,
Leon Litzky's firstborn son

Conscience, the uninvited guest . . .
—Aleksandr Sergeevich Pushkin

My conscience hath a thousand several tongues . . .
—King Richard in William Shakespeare's *Richard III*

FOREWORD

I HAVE TO OWN UP to a curious obsession: Lev Davidovich Bronshtein. Not his Marxist mindset, not his brutality during the 1918–22 Russian Civil War, not his blood feud with Josef Stalin or his forced exile in 1929 from the Soviet Union or, in 1940, his cold-blooded assassination, on Stalin's orders, in Mexican exile with an ice axe lodged in his brain. No, my obsession has its roots in Bronshtein's nom de guerre by which history, and the world, knows him: Leon Trotsky.

I'll explain: My father, born in America in 1896, was named Leon Litzky. In 1919 he applied to a judge in New York to change his family name to Littell. I have the legal papers in which he offered the judge a reason: My father claimed he was continually being held up to ridicule because his name, Leon Litzky, was similar to that of an infamous Russian revolutionist (as such people were called at the time) who lived in exile in the Bronx for ten weeks and two days before the 1917 Bolshevik Revolution, Leon Trotsky.

The judge must have stifled a smile when he granted my father's request. A New Yorker had to be oblivious not to know who Leon Trotsky was: At the tender age of twenty-six, leader of the world's first soviet ("council") during the short-lived 1905 Russian Revolution; later a Menshevik who joined the Bolsheviks and then became Lenin's alter ego, returning soon after him to Russia following the abdication of Czar Nicholas II; the fellow who actually organized the uprising that overthrew the post-czarist Provisional Government and put Lenin and his Bolsheviks—and eventually Stalin—in power, and later created and commanded the Red Army that defended the revolution during the brutal Russian Civil War.

Which is how my father and his two sons and his four grandsons and eight great-grandchildren wound up as Littells. And why I couldn't resist fantasizing about Trotsky's ten weeks and two days in New York before the 1917 Bolshevik Revolution.

The result is *Bronshtein in the Bronx.*

1

We will be Russians in America . . .

HERE'S THE THING: WHEN I was thirteen and a gangling yardbird in my father's pigsty, a dried turd's throw from the village of Yanofska in Ukraine's fertile steppe where the czarist arseholes permitted the occasional Jew to farm the farm he actually owned, I would set aside a fistful of minutes after evening chores to have a conversation with my smug conscience, whom I identified as a he because the voice in my mind's ear sounded suspiciously like the snarly rasp of my childhood nemesis Leon Litzky, the crippled classmate who broke his ankle kicking an extra point extra hard; the blood-spattered son of a bitch once attacked me with his wooden crutch when I refused to autograph the cast on his leg. My conscience, like Litzky, was a dyed-in-the-wool contrarian. If I said night, you could count on him saying day. If I opined that, given my natal horoscope, I was destined to become famous, he'd snap, his lower lip curling in contempt, that I was born under a shooting star and would definitely become infamous. If I argued the merits of permanent revolution (a notion already vexing my acne-scarred adolescence), Litzky's soundless laughter would tickle my ear as he claimed the only permanent things under the sun were the Russian Orthodox Church and Jew-baiting and masturbation, that and the grim reaper death. If I boasted of earning a second in the Realschule gymnasium in Odessa, I could hear his scornful snort in my ear. *Considering the competition, Bronshtein, you should have waltzed into a first.* When I reminded him that I didn't know how to waltz, he'd retort with a manic laugh, *Get a life, Bronshtein, learn to dance.*

I never did learn to dance.

On this particular Saturday morning, the thirteenth day of January in the third year of the Great War, 1917, as the coal-powered rust bucket of a tramp steamer *Montserrat*, seventeen days out of Barcelona, slowed to pick up the harbor pilot and then slipped past the Trojan horse the wily French offered to a naive America, I'm talking about the colossal statue of a female of the species misnamed Lady Liberty, I made the mistake of boasting I'd escaped from the czar's Siberian prisons not once but twice (the second time across a thousand miles of frozen tundra on a luge drawn by reindeer). My conscience, a tough cookie who flattered himself he was my better angel, whispered in my ear, *You escaped, Bronshtein, but you abandoned your wedded wife, Aleksandra Sokolovskaya, the mother of your two little girls, Ninushka and Zinushka, stranding all of them in Siberia to fend for themselves.*

The wife encouraged me to save myself, I protested. *The wife in question, an educated comrade who read Marx cover to cover before you knew the book existed, obviously loved the husband more than the husband loved the wife*, he retorted.

The wife in question, I explained, was reading an English translation of Ovid's "Remedies for Love"—which instructed women on how to fall *out* of love—and Aleksandra, taking her cue from this home-wrecker Ovid, announced that she had fallen out of love with me. She moved on so I moved out and on. All that is water under the bridge.

Hoping a change of subject would put the conversation onto more positive terrain, I mentioned that I was excited to be setting foot in the New World. Litzky, as incorrigible as a myopic mule, could barely swallow his exasperation. *Having been spit out of Russia and Austria and Switzerland and France and, more recently, Spain, of course you're excited to come to America. But is America excited to have a Menshevik like you—*

I cut him off to set the record straight: There was a time, I informed my nemesis Litzky, when I saw myself as the Menshevik, with a foot in both factions of the chronically befuddled Social Democratic Labor Party, who could reconcile the crabby Mensheviks with Vladimir Ilyich Lenin's cranky Bolsheviks and bring unity to the revolution that inhabits the old man's daydreams and nightmares. But I read the handwriting on the wall: We were wasting precious time and energy looking for unity. The war raging in Europe, the threat of President Wilson and the Americans joining in that war, the wilting of the czar if Russia should hopefully lose the war, required bold action, not shilly-shallying over commas and colons in a desperate quest for a middle ground. Truth is, I suspect I have become more comfortable identifying with Lenin's Bolsheviks than his Menshevik enemies. Despite his faults, I plunged on before my putative better angel could interrupt my interruption, despite his egomania, despite his explosive temper, despite his cantankerous rudeness and quarrelsome certitudes, despite his rancid breath and his squinting Mongolian eyes and the utter absence of a saving grace we identify as humor, Volodya—yes, yes, Lenin and I are on a first-name basis—Volodya, as I was saying, has the balls to get the lumpenproletariat off their collective asses. I admit we don't always see eye to eye—

Eye to eye! That's the understatement of the century. From the minute you looked up the exiled Bolshevik supremo in London—that was right after you escaped from Siberia in 1902, cap in hand you knocked on Lenin's door in Holford Square, if memory serves—you locked horns. You accused him to his face of being dictatorial, of not trusting the workers to bring Socialism to Russia. He called you a Judas and accused you of spouting puffed-up phrases arguing absurd theories. Hellfire, you loathed him last time the subject came up. The next to last time also.

I am having third thoughts, goddamn it. For Vladimir Lenin, revolution in Russia is an end; for me, it's bound to be contagious. But before we can argue about where and when the revolution ends, it has to begin. And if someone can rouse the lethargic Russian proletarian to revolution, who am I to quibble over bad breath. *Okay, okay, I stand corrected. But you don't answer the question, Bronshtein: Is America excited to have one of Lenin's clammy Bolsheviks wash up on its shores? Will they even let you in when they discover you are the famous—ha! I should say the infamous!—Leon Trotsky hoping to ignite the fuse to world revolution here in America?*

God's nails, enough's enough: This keen as mustard conscience of mine had a genius for getting my goat. I could tell when he got my goat because my teeth hurt. Right now, my teeth ached. In a panic—I had made my way to the vestibule of the New World hoping to start again from scratch—I told my nemesis Litzky to piss the hell off. And off he sulkily pissed, leaving me with the illusion that brought me to the New World: That revolution in America might just be imaginable.

And imagine it I did. That isn't so much another story as the heart and soul and gut and prostate and intestines and testicles of this story. I even fantasized about the headline: RUSSIAN JEW TROTSKY IGNITES SOCIALIST FUSE IN CAPITALIST AMERICA.

If only.

Litzky's singsong *Will they even let you in?* rang in my ears. As much as it distressed me to admit it, my conscience had a point. I had made it past security to board the *Montserrat* in Barcelona, along with my longtime companion and bedmate,

Natalya Sedova, and our two sons, nine-year-old Sergei and eleven-year-old Lyova, using counterfeit documents in the name of Zratsky, Sergei, that listed my occupation as writer, which is more or less how I had managed to keep food on the table since being expelled from Russia ten years before. Several of the articles I filed from the Balkan Front for a small Russian émigré newspaper had been picked up by leading French and German dailies, and though the byline credited "from wire dispatches" and not the war correspondent Leon Trotsky, the embarrassingly trivial sum they paid for reprint rights eventually trickled down to yours truly. The brutal Balkan War had, I am the first to admit, left its mark on me. I still associate the smell of tobacco with lice—soldiers, refugees, journalists like me took to sprinkling precious tobacco on their clothing to get rid of the typhus-bearing lice. I still have the occasional nightmare of visiting hospital wards swarming with young soldiers with self-inflicted wounds—they would shoot off a finger or a toe, careful to fire the bullet through a loaf of stale bread so as not to leave telltale powder burns on the wound.

I could feel the deck plates vibrating under the worn soles of my boots as the *Montserrat* backed its engines and eased up to Pier 8 on the river east of Manhattan Island. We could hear the muffled shouts of sailors winching in lines. Sergei, in his stockinged feet, climbed onto his bunk to peer out the porthole and gaze in wide-eyed open-mouthed wonder at the mountain range of buildings silhouetted against the yellowish gleam seeping like a smog over Manhattan.

"Come look, Papa," he exclaimed. "Some of the buildings must be twelve stories high—oh my gosh, they're scraping the bottom of the sky."

"Resist the temptation to be whelmed by tall buildings," I said. "They are built on the skeletons of workers. And they can be a pain in the neck, literally, if you gape too long at the roofs."

"Papa, is it so that we waste one-third of our life sleeping?"

"There are some who say we waste two-thirds of our life awake."

"Who's right?"

"Depends."

"Depends on what?"

"What you're doing during the two-thirds you're awake."

"And what should we be doing?"

"You should be making revolution."

"What's revolution, Papa?"

"Lev!" Natalya exclaimed.

Over the loudspeaker the ship's bells sounded the hour. "Six bells," Lyova said brightly. "What time is that, Papa?" When I told him it was three in the morning, he laughed uneasily. "My gosh, I've never been up this late!"

"Three in the morning is so late it's early," I remarked. I savored the delicious sensation of threading my fingers through my son's frizzy hair. "*Rannyaya ptashka lovit chervyaka*—it's the early bird that catches the worm," I reminded him.

"I don't eat worms." Lyova was worried that his failure to eat worms would annoy me. "I am planning to be a vegetarian when I grow up," he told me.

"If you grow up," I said.

"Bite your tongue, Lev," Natalya said under her breath.

"Me, also, I don't eat worms, Papa," Sergei declared brightly.

"Our children don't eat worms," I informed Natalya with a straight face.

"Thank the lord for small miracles," she muttered.

"Will we be American in America?" Lyova asked.

"We are Russian," I instructed him. "We will be Russian in America."

"Why are you smiling, Lev?" Natalya, buckling the belts on the boys' canvas grips, asked me.

"I am smiling because I finally worked up the nerve to tell my conscience to"—I mouthed the next words—"piss off."

"Father is cursing again?" Lyova exclaimed. "When he mouths words he is usually saying naughty things that he doesn't want us to hear."

"Are we still the Zratsky family, Papa?" Sergei wanted to know.

"I prefer Trotsky," Lyova insisted proudly.

"I prefer Bronshtein," Natalya said, "but as Lady Liberty discovered brandishing her torch to light the way for immigrants coming to America, nobody takes females seriously."

"I take females seriously," I corrected her inasmuch as

what she said needed correction, "if they are committed to world revolution. Your Lady Liberty is a fairy tale marketing American exceptionalism. American exceptionalism, which is American hubris by another name, is the unspoken justification for American exploitation of the rest of the civilized world."

"What does exception-ism mean, Papa?" Sergei asked.

"Exceptionalism is a theory that holds that American capitalism constitutes an exception to the economic laws governing national historical development."

Impossible to miss the specter of a fleeting smile on Natalya's pale lips. "For pity's sake, Lev," she snapped impatiently, "he's nine years old!"

"When I was nine years old—"

Natalya pressed an editor's forefinger to my lips. "I wasn't born yesterday," she said. "The Lev Bronshtein I've slept with for more years than I can count was never nine years old."

The ego-addict Litzky couldn't resist putting in his two cents. *That's my take, too, Bronshtein. When the other boys in your tumbledown Yanofska boondock were playing fleas-in-a-bowl, you were concocting a less conventional storyline—you turned your back on the Jewish yardbird and, like an actor stumbling onto a stage, reinvented yourself as an ur-revolutionist.*

Goddamn it, I believed in revolution, I saw it, like that great proletarian stationmaster Karl Marx, as the locomotive of history—

You believed in revolution because you decided it was one of the few ways a Russian Jew could grab the undivided attention of the world.

Your problem, Comrade Litzky, is that you're addicted to ulterior motives—you freak out if you don't get a daily fix. Here's the thing: In the beginning there might have been—. Okay, okay, let's agree there was a grain of truth in what you say. But my two stints in the czar's Siberian icebox turned the half-hearted union organizer Bronshtein into a passionate revolutionist. What I'm saying is that I not only believed in the need for violence that goes by the name of revolution, I lived it.

I thought I could hear Litzky, who didn't take kindly to being contradicted, applauding. *You still haven't figured it out, have you, Bronshtein. You may have convinced yourself that you believed it. But attention is what you craved before you were old enough to jack off. Also after.*

Do you absolutely have to poison every conversation with your Freudian bullshit? I demanded.

Yo, my man Bronshtein—feel free to turn me off the way you flicked off the newfangled wind-up Victrola in the Montserrat *cafeteria playing over and over the single record they possessed—which happened to be a favorite of mine, Rachmaninoff's Piano Concerto no. 2 with the maestro himself tickling the ivories. Go ahead, Bronshtein—I dare you. Ha! I thought so. You won't shut down your better angel because having a conscience whispering in your ear permits you to feel morally superior.*

Natalya looked up worriedly. "You frighten me, Lev, talking to him all the time."

"I frighten myself, but I can't kick the habit; in my head I hear the raving of my busted-ankle nemesis Leon Litzky, who deludes himself into thinking he's my better angel." I took a deep breath. "There are days I wish I'd never gotten in touch with my conscience. But all things considered—"

Finish the thought, Bronshtein. Natalya is hanging on your every word. Me, also. All things considered?

"All things considered, a conscience is a handy amigo when you're trying to sleepwalk your way through this pea soup fog we identify as life."

Screw you, Bronshtein.

"Screw me," I agreed.

"Daaaad!" the boys cried in mortified chorus.

Jamming the pince-nez onto the bridge of my nose, I retrieved the Russian passports in the name of Bronshtein stashed under the lining of one of our suitcases. Each passport was printed on a sheaf of ornate stationery engraved with the imperial eagle. "If anyone asks, kindly remember we are the Bronshtein family," I instructed the boys. "I doubt very much the immigration inspectors, serving life sentences inside the fortress of their American exceptionalism, will recognize the name. Repeat your names, if you please," I told the boys.

"Bronshtein, Lyova."

"Bronshtein, Sergei."

"I, too, shall use my real name, Sedova, Natalya, and I am thrilled you three will be entering America as Bronshteins," Natalya said. She favored me with one of her sideways looks. "At least comb your hair before you set foot in the New World, for pity's sake," she said. "You'll give Russian revolutionists a bad name looking like a disheveled tramp."

"Nata, my love, my victim, this is my hair combed," I protested as I pulled my thick knee socks up to the elastic of my knickerbockers and double knotted the laces of my ankle boots.

Natalya fetched my German worker's cap from her shoulder satchel. "Could have fooled me," she said, and she laughed that edgy laugh of hers that had more impatience than humor in it.

2

You came to the wrong country . . .

NATALYA, LYOVA, SERGEI AND YOUR servant, Litzky's man Bronshtein, my Serbian army surplus duffel (a relic of months reporting on the ruthless Balkan War) and two bags at our feet, happened to wind up in line directly ahead of two American merchant sailors whose ship had been torpedoed by a German submarine and were hitching a ride back to the U.S. on the *Montserrat.* The younger of the two, with a stubble of a goatee on his pointed chin, broke the awkward silence and blurted out to everyone within earshot that they were lucky to be alive. "Our ship had a cargo of two thousand horses and mules," he confided as if he were conveying top secret war department information. "We managed to swing out the longboat and save ourselves, but there was a terrifying nightmare behind us. Jesus, Mary and Joseph, the sight of them horses and mules thrashing around in the sea—the sound of their frantic whinnying as they drowned—will haunt me for the rest of my livelong days."

"Kindly spare us the sickening details," Nata said sharply, "lest you give me nightmares too."

I was wearing what Nata called my armor: The stiff sealskin coat that I'd bought secondhand in a Paris flea market and used as bedding on endless train trips across Europe, along with the scarf Nata had fashioned for me from a fraying silk slip that, as it had been worn next to her skin, reeked of eroticism. Nata was bundled into her thick cloth coat with the fur collar so threadbare it looked as if the animal had grown bald before it was slaughtered. The boys were dressed, like me, in corduroy knickerbockers and itchy knee-length mountain socks, along with the belted cloth winter coats that we'd splurged on in Paris. "Papa," Sergei whined, poking me to get my attention, "are we almost there?"

I could hear Litzky mumbling in my ear, *You certain the customs agents won't connect Bronshtein with Trotsky?*

The only thing I'm really certain of is the date, I told myself. And in a voice that resonated in the cabin, I announced, "It's Saturday, the thirteenth of January, in the year of the Lord 1917."

"Year of our Lord!" Nata exclaimed. "The next thing you know you'll replace your worker's cap with a yarmulka. And why for heaven's sake are you announcing the date?" she inquired. "Please don't tell me you have nothing better to do than yabber away with that devil of a conscience of yours."

"I have nothing better to do," I teased to get Nata's goat.

Judging from the glacial gleam in her gorgeous green eyes, her goat is what I got.

Scratching at a shaggy sideburn trickling down his ruddy Irish cheekbone, the policeman directing traffic at the door of the dining hall called out, "Next, now."

That's you, my man Bronshtein, Litzky prodded. *You're next.*

Carrying the duffel and one of our bags, I made my way across the ship's first-class dining room, its picture windows streaming tears of condensation, to the thin young man with a high forehead holding fort behind a table. He was wearing a bow tie, the first I'd ever seen on a live male of the species, and sucking on a foul-smelling cigarillo. He didn't look up when I plunked down our four passports. A wooden nameplate identified him as JOHN E. HOOVER, BUREAU OF INVESTIGATION. Plucking the cigarillo from his mouth, he finally deigned to glance at me. "Which one of these passports is yours?" he wanted to know. With my palm I flattened the one with my picture on it. The young man absently waved a hand to dispel the cigarillo smoke and leaned over the document to read my name. "Bronshtein, Lev," he muttered to himself. He ran a thick index finger down the ship's manifest. "Funny thing, there doesn't seem to be a Bronshtein on the passenger list," he noted. "Could that be because you boarded the ship in Barcelona using the name Zratsky, Sergei?" Scrutinizing me through the swirling smoke with eyes shot with blood, he said, "Welcome to America, Mr. Trotsky, a.k.a. Zratsky, a.k.a. Bronshtein."

I will admit that I was startled when I heard him use the name Trotsky. "Bronshtein is my father's name, and mine," I insisted.

A jaded smile contaminated by contempt clawed its way onto Mr. Hoover's delicate lips. "Correct me if I'm wrong: Bronshtein is an Israelite name."

You're on thin ice, Litzky murmured in my ear. *Something tells me he doesn't hold Jews in high esteem.*

Mr. Hoover flipped open a file folder and produced a copy of the *New York Call.* He pushed the newspaper across the table so I could read the headline. The front page had a photograph of me and the headline DRIVEN OUT OF EUROPE, LEON TROTSKY TAKES UP WORK AS A RADICAL WRITER HERE. Hoover barely managed to suppress a smirk as he relished my discomfort. "Yes, yes, you see we know who you are, Mr. Trotsky, Leon. Our Bureau of Investigation agents have been collecting string on you—we know your age and your height and your weight and the color of your eyes, we know you're allergic to pollen and peanuts, we know you are right-handed and, ideologically speaking, slightly to the left of your Vladimir Ulyanov, a.k.a. Lenin. Tell me, out of curiosity, however did Bronshtein come up with the name Trotsky?"

"The original Trotsky was a prison guard in Odessa—he was more of a human being than the judges who sentenced me, in my ten-minute trial, to live in Siberia for the rest of my life. I sign my articles Trotsky. It's my nom de plume and my nom de guerre, depending on whether I'm writing or fighting."

"We are not at war here in America—yet—though if President Wilson has his way, and German submarines keep sinking our merchantmen, we will join the European war soon enough. So for the moment you have no need of a nom de guerre." Laughing under his breath at his own drollness, Hoover flattened Natalya's passport. "The woman traveling with you is not a Bronshtein. Is Natalya Ivanovna Sedova your lawful wedded wife who, like these sexless suffragettes, prefers to keep her maiden name rather than adopt her husband's name?"

"She is the unlawful unwedded mother of my sons."

"You came to the wrong country," John E. Hoover said. "This is still, thanks to God, Puritan America, Mr. Trotsky, Leon. Flaunting a mistress is frowned on." He inked his stamp on a pad, then breathed onto it and brought it down hard on each of our four passport papers. I retrieved the papers and folded them into an inside pocket of my sealskin coat.

Litzky's sour breath tickled my ear. *Go ahead, ask him, for Pete's sake. He stamped the passports, what do you have to lose?*

Egged on by my self-proclaimed better angel, I plunged. "Mind if I ask you a question, Mr. Hoover? If you and your Bureau of Investigation are convinced I'm a threat to your Puritan America, why are you letting me in?"

Excellent question, Litzky said with an appreciative snicker. *You have balls after all.*

Mr. Hoover sat back in his chair, sucking on his cigarillo, eyeing the ash sprouting at the end of it with a distinctly glassy stare. "Excellent question," he allowed. "You have balls after all"—and for a terrifying instant I wondered if Mr. Hoover's Bureau of Investigation was able to eavesdrop on my conversations with Litzky. "I suppose there's no harm in my telling you," he went on, "inasmuch as the Jew press has spelled it out in an editorial welcoming you to New York. Right now our homegrown Socialists are obsessed with working hours and salaries and—I try not to hoot when I say this—paid vacations. What they're not obsessed with is revolution. Some genius who is above my pay grade decided if we could radicalize the Socialist kingpins, that would be the end of them—they would be mocked off the stage when they tried to persuade the rank and file to mutiny. Americans may dream of higher wages and a forty-hour work week and paid vacations, but they're uncomfortable with evolution and they dread revolution. Americans, Mr. Trotsky, are happy with America as it is. You, with your willy-nilly appeals to riot, will inoculate our working class and keep them that way. But I suggest you watch your butt. If you so much as cross the street against the light you will wind up cleaning latrines in one of our prisons."

"I have seen the inside of prisons in my life," I reminded him. "I've cleaned more toilets than I've shat in."

I wasn't sure he heard me. "If worse comes to worst," Mr. Hoover was saying, "you can always make use of your nom de plume to write an article comparing our American prisons to your Russian prisons." Mr. Hoover wasn't finished with me. "Make no mistake," he said, his voice reduced to a hoarse growl that had a lot in common with the stifled bark of a dog, "if it was up to me, godless anarchists like you who preach the violent destruction of our American way of life would be on the first boat back to Russia."

"My good luck that it isn't up to you."

3

The thing I like most is the foxtrot . . .

THE ICINESS OF THE AIR stung my nostrils and fogged my pince-nez as I stepped out on deck. Streetlamps and headlamps stabbed through the predawn murkiness to sling shadows in every direction. An ancient lady wearing an army greatcoat several sizes too large was scattering what looked like breadcrumbs on a loading ramp as seagulls screamed their appreciation over her head. Lugging my duffel and one of our suitcases down the gangway, checking to be sure Nata and the boys were behind me, I could hear the high-pitched whinny of horses tied to lampposts on the street beyond the pier—it pleased me to imagine they were protesting equine exploitation by capitalist stable owners. The whinnying brought to mind my father's favorite Russian proverb, the one where a conquering Mongol complains about not having stirrups—which, when I thought about it, seemed to sum up my predicament in America. In the fading darkness, I realized there was a crowd on Pier 8, thirty, maybe forty people, stamping their feet to keep the frost from biting, exhaling small clouds of frost into the icy morning air with each breath, and I wondered who they had come to welcome until it dawned on me that they had come to welcome me.

"There he is!"

"Mr. Trotsky!"

"Over here, Mr. Trotsky!"

"Could you give us an I'm-thrilled-to-be-in-America smile, please, Leon."

Flashbulbs exploded as the first pale rays of sunlight grazed the pier's pylons. Someone at the bottom of the gangway was holding up a copy of the Russian-language newspaper *Novy Mir* and I could make out my photograph on the front page and a headline, IN COMRADE TROTSKY, AMERICA GAINS A RESOLUTE FIGHTER FOR THE REVOLUTIONARY INTERNATIONAL.

Litzky was in high spirits. *Americans obviously have a weakness for Russians who escape from one of the czar's Siberian country clubs.*

My alter ego's enthusiasm was contagious. As I set foot on the pier, Lenin's Finnish comrade Aleksandra Kollontai, looking more beautiful than I remembered in an elegant velvet robe with a gold chain around her swan's neck, thrust a bouquet of wilted roses into my hand and shouted out a mantra I later discovered came from a headline in the *New Yorker Volkszeitung*, "Leon Trotsky *Kommt Heute*!" My spirits soared: Despite the John E. Hoovers weeding out invasive rhizomes in the vestibule of the New World, despite my shaggy Mongol pony not being equipped with stirrups as I set out to drain the capitalist swamp, Socialist revolution might be possible in North America after all. And if we could ignite Socialist revolution in one country, any country—Russia, Germany, England, America, it couldn't have mattered less which—the revolution would spread across the globe like a pandemic producing variants. Revolution would be permanent.

Permanent revolution, that was the ticket.

A man I recognized pushed past Aleksandra to greet me—it was the young Bolshevik Nikolai Bukharin with his red beard and a jubilant horselaugh forever on the tip of his tongue. We had lived a stone's throw from one another when we were both exiled to Vienna; my Natalya had become good friends with his wife, Nadezhda Mikhailovna. I dropped my duffel and the bag and caught him up in a bear hug. "What are you doing here, Bukharin?" I cried to be heard over the crowd.

"The New World is broken, comrade," he said with an ear-to-ear grin. "I came to join you in repairing America."

Reporters were shouting questions. "Mr. Trotsky, would you share with us your first impression of America?"

"Happy to: I noticed that your illustrious Statue of Liberty presides over the entrance to New York with her back turned to the rest of the country, which I took to mean she has rejected your capitalist system."

"Can you tell us what you like most about America, Mr. Trotsky?"

I recollected my conscience's *Get a life, Bronshtein, learn to dance.* "Well, I've been in America for all of five minutes, but I can say the thing I like most is the foxtrot." *You're being too glib*, Litzky warned sulkily. *Give them something to chew on.* "To answer you seriously," I added, speaking slowly so the journalists could take notes, "when this European war, which is being fought by workers on both ends of the bayonet, finally ends, the proletariat will demand an accounting from their capitalist masters, and the resulting social riot will eclipse anything the earth has so far seen."

A young woman wearing a gentleman's flannel trousers, a coal black thigh-length redingote bedizened with colorful military ribbons and a flaming-red sailor's watch cap waved to get my attention. "Fédora, from the *Brooklyn Daily Eagle*," she shouted. "Hey, the Russian Empire has a population of a hundred twenty-five million, Mr. Lenin's Bolsheviks boast a membership of twenty-five thousand. Explain, please, if you are able to, Mr. Trotsky, how you propose to organize a revolution when you are so outnumbered."

I thought I detected a slight rolling of *r*'s in her pronunciation of my name and the word "revolution," suggesting that she wasn't born in America, and called over the heads of the crowd, "Where are you from?"

"I'm from here, from Brooklyn."

"You weren't always from Brooklyn, judging by the way the *r*'s roll off your tongue."

"You have a good ear, Mr. Trotsky. That's because I'm half Me-hi-can. Not to mention half Jewish. Not to mention half *Eagle* newshawk and half émigré like you."

"Is there anything you're not half of?" I inquired.

"Woman," Fédora shot back. She stabbed strands of hair away from her eyes. "Even dressed like a man, I am all woman. But you don't answer my question, Mr. Trotsky."

She's cute! But don't get any ideas, Bronshtein—remember how Natalya looked daggers at you when you chatted up that girl in Berlin.

"You put the question backward, Miss Fédora. How can one hundred twenty-five million bourgeois prevent a revolution made by twenty-five thousand idealists who are ready to risk their lives to change the world? History, Miss Half-Journalist from the *Brooklyn Daily Eagle*, is driven by passionate, idea-focused minorities."

The young woman angled her head skeptically. "And can you honestly say you swallow your own theory?"

"Depending on the hour of the day, or the day of the week, and my appetite at any given moment, I try to."

That drew a laugh from the crowd. *Resist your instinct to come across as a stand-up comic, Bronshtein,* my conscience cautioned. *Keep in mind that you are a world-famous upsetter of applecarts and act like one.*

"What about revolution in these forty-eight states of

North America?" a disheveled young man shouted. "Do you think it's a pipe dream?"

"Excuse me but I do not understand the expression 'pipe dream.' Are you suggesting revolution is the dream of a pipe?"

The young man started to explain when an older man at the back of the crowd cut him off. "A pipe dream is what Weltanschauung-politicians like Trotsky here—windbags intoxicated with the notion that ends justify means who celebrate the cruel carnival that goes by the name of revolution—offer a naive working class."

Half a dozen women nearest the older man closed in on him. "For shame, for shame," several of them cried menacingly until the older man, shrugging, backed away and, turning, walked away.

"Ends, my friends," I called out, addressing my words to the crowd more than the retreating man who had been taunting me, "justify means if they are world changing."

Miss Fédora's hand shot up. "Does the 1905 Russian revolution come back to haunt you with what could have been?"

Natalya tugged at my arm. "The boys are cold," she said.

"Just a minute more," I told her and turned back to the crowd. "No, Miss Fédora from the *Brooklyn Daily Eagle*, the 1871 Paris Commune, with its red flags and barricades and massacred revolutionists and its pipe dream"—using the new expression gave me a measure of satisfaction—"yes, yes, its pipe dream of a people's republic haunts 1905 with what could have been."

Nikolai Bukharin and Aleksandra Kollontai began to clap their hands in agreement. Several people around them took up the applause and in the bat of an eyelash everyone who had come to greet me was laughing and applauding. "*Uraaa*, Trotsky," the crowd cried in jubilant chorus.

In the Russian style, I applauded back.

Try to resist getting a swelled head, Litzky cautioned me.

Too late, I muttered.

4

Dzhugashvili has adopted the nom de guerre Stalin . . .

IN MY MIND'S EYE, THE next hours came to resemble one of those Pathé News clips we saw in a Paris cinema—only sped up so that days later, when everyone calmed down, I had trouble remembering in what order things happened. Still, I shall try to construct our first hours and days in New York as best I can. Nikolai Bukharin had organized a hotel for our first night in the New World. At Pier 8 we all squeezed into a yellow taxicab, the boys sitting on laps, that took us past the Metropolitan Life Insurance Tower with the giant clock on its face, along with department stores named Macy's and Gimbels and Lord & Taylor, to the Hotel Astor, a posh hotel in Manhattan's Times Square between Forty-Fourth and Forty-Fifth Streets. The building, down the block from an enormous gaudy sign advertising scantily clad Ziegfeld Girls (which Nata found vulgar), was eleven stories high—the boys stood on the sidewalk craning their necks as they counted the floors. Hotel Astor turned out to have an opulent lobby, with crystal light fixtures on the walls and frescoes painted on the ceiling. I spotted a billiard room off to one side and heard soft piano music wafting in from the bar. And then there was the army of valets dressed in what Nata took to be military parade uniforms—two of them took charge of my duffel and our two bags and sped us up in an enormous elevator fitted with mirrors to a sumptuous suite of rooms on the eighth floor.

"Who's paying for all this?" I whispered to Bukharin when I saw him tipping the valets.

"Don't worry your head, Trotsky—the Party is footing the bill for your first night in New York."

The boys ran screeching through the three rooms and the white tiled bathroom, throwing all the light switches on and testing the taps in the kitchen alcove and the bathroom. "Papa," Sergei cried, "you are not going to believe this but the water runs hot or cold depending on which faucet you open."

Bukharin, who was ten years younger and half a head shorter than me, took me down to the bar for a much-needed drink as Nata and the boys settled in. "Two vodkas, and kindly make sure the glasses are iced," he instructed the barmaid as we slid into a plush leather booth. The drinks appeared, along with a bowl filled with something the Americans call pretzels. "*Zdorov'ya*, Trotsky," Bukharin exclaimed and we clanked glasses and downed the vodka, Russian style, in one long gulp. He signaled the bar girl for a refill.

I leaned closer and lowered my voice. "What news from the comrades, Bukharin?"

"The old man hasn't changed," he told me, shaking his head. "He is not comfortable with honest disagreement. The hard fact is that Lenin has difficulty tolerating anyone with brains."

I had to smile. "So you came to America not to escape the czarist police—you came to put some distance between you and Lenin."

Bukharin's raucous laughter filled the bar. The piano player as well as several men drinking at the back of the room glanced at us. ("Russians," I heard one of them explain to his tablemates.) "When it comes to ideological matters," Bukharin went on, obviously relieved to get some things off his chest, "the old man has a lot in common with the pope in Rome—he speaks ex cathedra. His views—on revolution, on the dictatorship of the proletariat, on the postcapitalist withering away of the state, on Marx's thesis-antithesis-synthesis formulation—come from the thigh of Jupiter. Christ, how Lenin loves to bicker. He and I argued late into the night, the night before I left Austria, about the Bolsheviks' role as the vanguard of the revolution—whether, in short, we led the proletariat or followed the proletariat."

"And what did you say?"

"I argued that we had to follow—without masses of workers and army mutineers leading the way, we would be crushed by the czar's police. It would be Bloody Sunday 1905 redux."

"What news from that crazy Georgian who robs banks and sends Lenin valises filled with rubles?" I inquired.

"Dzhugashvili? He let it be known that he has adopted the nom de guerre Stalin. As he never makes the mistake of arguing with Lenin, the old man trusts him. Hold on to your seat, Trotsky—Lenin assigned Dzhugashvili to write a paper on the role of nationalism in a postrevolutionary Russia. This Stalin may be the only authentic peasant in Lenin's inner circle of coffeehouse intellectuals, me among them—but he is totally uneducated, or educated in an Orthodox seminary, which is the same as being uneducated. His father is said to be a drunken bootmaker in Gori. Look, it's one thing to rob banks and put a bullet between the eyes of your rivals, it's quite another to put two coherent sentences on the sticky question of nationalism back-to-back. Dzhugashvili is consumed by ambition—he is said to be obsessed with Ivan the Terrible, whom he thinks of as a role model—but my gut tells me he'll burn out if Lenin asks too much of the Georgian's brain."

"I heard a rumor that this Dzhugashvili has Ossete bandit blood in his veins," I told Bukharin.

He thought about this for a moment. "If what they say is true," he said with a half laugh that surely left a bitter taste on his tongue, "he's ruthless enough to wind up spilling an ocean of blood should Lenin ever put him into a position of power."

We drank off the second vodka in silence. "I hope you're not worn out by your arrival, Trotsky," Bukharin said. "I'm trying to organize a dinner in Brooklyn with several important Socialists. You'll see what we're up against when we talk revolution to them."

"I'm running on what our modern medical mavens have identified as adrenaline," I told him.

5

Papa, come look—there's a bathtub . . .

WHEN BUKHARIN FIRST PRONOUNCED THE word "Bronques," I thought he was talking about a canton in the Balkans. Accredited to a Russian newspaper, I'd covered the war there, the bloody ethnic sanitizing of the Albanians by the Serbs that the world knows as the 1912 Balkan War, and though I didn't consider myself squeamish, I still suffered from terrifying flashes of hindsight: I had, as my conscience remembered all too well, watched them dragging limbless, decapitated Albanian bodies from a bombed train. I had used my newfangled Eastman Kodak bellows camera to photograph the bloated bodies of two drowned children that had washed up from a strafed whaleboat—they were still clinging one to the other, each undoubtedly hoping that the other could somehow save her. I had been on hand when the Swiss Croix Rouge nurses in their blood-starched white dresses discovered a shallow mass grave after a torrential overnight rain had washed the earth away from the 278 corpses—I counted them whilst the nurses and my not-so-tough cookie of a conscience averted their eyes. Each corpse had a pencil-thin bullet hole in the back of his neck. *The both of us had better get hardened to the sight of mass graves and bloated bodies*, Litzky had chided me at the time. *Because that's what we'll have to live with if you succeed in inciting revolution. Millions will lose their lives when you lose your innocence.*

I won't flinch, I remember promising myself: Revolutions are verbose, that's sure and certain, and it's no secret that revolutions are also brutal—witness the dozens of thousands slaughtered by Monsieur Guillotin's contraption that was supposed to make executions more humane. Still, as long as some ends can be said to justify some means, and the particular end in question is a worker's and peasant's utopia, I'm ready to live with the consequences. For me, revolution is the name of the game.

"It's spelled B-r-o-n-x," Bukharin educated me as the five of us climbed the steps to the Third Avenue Elevated at the Forty-Second Street station. "And the last time I looked it was not in the Balkans," he added with a belly laugh that had other fares depositing their nickels and pushing through turnstiles glancing in our direction. My boys had been in the metro in Paris, but the trip uptown on the New York Elevated bedazzled them. Nata, sitting on a long wooden bench, did her level best to look blasé, but Sergei and Lyova, kneeling on either side of her so they could gape out the window, couldn't suppress their squeals of excitement. As we were traveling during what the Americans called rush hour, the wagon quickly filled with passengers and cigarette smoke. At 129th Street, we caught a glimpse of the Harlem River, with barges offloading at its wooden docks. "That's the Bronx ahead," Bukharin told us, pointing, as the train rounded a curve, at the neat rows of one-story houses on either side of a dirt road. We got off at 174th Street and made our way past a poultry farm and, farther on, a push-cart filled with beetroots, to a five-story corner apartment building on Vyse Avenue, number 1522, where, thanks to a friend of Bukharin's, we had rented a three-room flat for $18 a month. As the flat came unfurnished, Bukharin had organized beds and window shades and a cast-off couch, along with chairs and tables (one for the kitchen, one for me to use as a desk) from Henry Feuer's Bronx furniture shop for $2 a week.

"What I love best is the garbage chute in the hallway," Sergei yelled breathlessly from the door of the apartment.

"Papa, come look—there's a bathtub!" Lyova called from the lavatory.

Bukharin was extolling the virtues of the neighborhood to my companion. "There are grocery stores around the corner on Tremont Avenue, and public schools for the boys, as well as the Bronx Zoo, all within walking distance."

Nata—who had seen the inside of czarist jails in her time—tested the gas jets on the stove, then raised the kitchen shade to let the sun stream in through the window.

Standing with her back to the sun, which turned her blouse transparent, she delivered her verdict. "This will do nicely. Don't you agree, Lev?"

I wasn't convinced. Taking Bukharin aside, I told him in an undertone, "It's a fine flat, bigger than the one we had in Paris that had a toilet on the landing between floors. But eighteen dollars a month! Plus the eight dollars for the furniture makes twenty-six dollars a month, not counting food and nickels for the New York Elevated. How on earth am I going to make ends meet?"

Cheapskate, the voice in my ear sneered.

I lost my rag: Piss off, Litzky! A cheapskate is someone who has a lot of money and worries about spending it. I have almost no money and worry about not having enough to put food on the table.

Bukharin raised an inquisitive eyebrow. "Who the hell are you talking to?"

"Myself."

"To answer your question," Bukharin said. "We're four blocks from the Third Avenue Elevated, which goes all the way to Greenwich Village in lower Manhattan."

"And what, pray tell, is in Greenwich Village?" I inquired.

Bukharin produced one of his trademark belly laughs. "*Novy Mir* is in Greenwich Village," he said, as if it explained everything. "*Novy Mir* is how you will make ends meet."

6

Revolution is what brings me to America . . .

HERE'S THE THING: *NOVY MIR*, a Russian-language broadsheet that despite its small circulation (8,000 on a good day) was the heart and soul and flame of Bolshevism in America, did explain everything. The editor in chief, Gregory Weinstein, happened to be an old pal from the short-lived 1905 Saint Petersburg riot—I suppose I ought to get used to calling this pearl of a city by its new Russified name, Petrograd—that almost but not quite mushroomed into a full-fledged revolution; a multitude had marched on the czar's Winter Palace demanding a constitution, wielding sabers the czar's Cossacks had charged and a river of blood had dyed the cobblestones red on what became known as Bloody Sunday. At the still green-behind-the-ears age of twenty-six, I wound up as chairman of Russia's first-ever soviet; like me, Gregory was arrested and sentenced to a penal colony in Siberia but, with his habitual resourcefulness, escaped in ten days and made his way to Paris and, eventually, New York. I could see he hadn't changed much since our paths last crossed: He was still thin as a scallion, with an imposing beard that looked as if it hadn't been washed or combed or trimmed anytime recently. "Lev Davidovich!" he exclaimed when I crossed the threshold of 77 Saint Marks Place, a dirty brownstone with a dentist's shingle upstairs and *Novy Mir*—New World—one flight down in Dante's basement purgatory. "Welcome to these occasionally-united states of America. You are a sight for my soul-sore eyes."

And for the first time since debarking on Pier 8, I did feel welcome in the United States of America. For Gregory's three small rooms in the basement on Saint Marks Place—with desks and filing cabinets crammed into every nook and cranny, with Russian posters taped to the peeling paint on the walls, with cigarette ends spilling out of overfull ashtrays and cabbage soup cooking on the tabletop gas burner next to the linotype machine and the printing press—gave me the comfortable sensation of having put one foot back into my much-beloved Russia.

I couldn't miss Litzky's snort of derision in my mind's ear. *You have a convenient forgettery, Bronshtein—what you liked best about Gregory's shoestring operation was he agreed to pay you $20 a week for writing columns in his pretend newspaper, its eight pages stuffed with so many adverts for Budweiser beer and neighborhood banks you had to peer through the cracks between the ads to find a scrap of news.*

As usual, I scolded my erstwhile conscience, you exaggerate—the ads are surely what make ends meet at *Novy Mir*. As for the $20, that was my safety net, and a safety net is not to be sneezed at, I don't deny it, but what I liked most was Gregory's "jailbird reunion," the phrase he used when he introduced me to his staff. You'll forgive me if I don't get into a tedious back-and-forth with you, Litzky, I said, and cutting short the dialogue with my conscience, I settled into a seat at the desk next to Bukharin's and, on the spot, turned out a column that appeared in the following morning's edition under the headline LONG LIVE THE STRUGGLE.

"So, Trotsky, tell me what really brings you to America," Gregory, nursing a tall glass of draft beer, demanded. We were on our lunch break and he had taken me to the Monopole Café on Second Avenue, which he described as a hangout for unemployed actors and unpublished writers and untalented portrait painters. Two young men with shoulder-length hair were playing chess at a table near the double door to the kitchen, two others dressed in coveralls were looking on over their shoulders.

"In a word, revolution is what brings me to America."

"Revolution?" Gregory appeared startled. "Where?"

"Here."

"You have to be pulling my leg, my dear Trotsky. Revolution in America! I can see you haven't been in the country long enough to test the temperature of the water. Right now it is ice-cold."

"Surely the Socialists can light a fire under the underpaid, underfed, underprivileged masses," I said. And I tried one of my lecture-tested clichés on him: "A handful of idealists ready to risk their lives to change the world—"

Swallowing a laugh, Gregory cut me off. "American Socialists are a miserable fraction of the population, Trotsky. At the first hint of an uprising, the Bureau of Investigation, the Pinkertons, the National Guard, the New York Police will round up the rabble-rousers and lock them in jails and throw away the keys." He drank off a draught of beer, then blotted the foam on his lips with the back of a sleeve. "You need to do your homework, Trotsky. American Socialists are obsessed with one thing: Improving American capitalism."

"But you edit *Novy Mir*!" I exclaimed. "Your newspaper blows on the embers, keeping them alive. Surely you can see a way forward to revolution."

Gregory thought about this. "I make it my business to deal with realities, not pipe dreams," he finally said. "You and I are marooned in America, but we must look to Russia for revolution. We need to transform the energy of the World War into proletarian anger, then transform proletarian anger into revolution. Russia, thank God, is losing this bloody war against Germany. The czar goes to great lengths to hide the truth, but truth has a way of outing: It is said that millions of Russian peasants have been killed or wounded, and masses of them have deserted. I have heard that the Germans stack the bodies of Russian soldiers in front of their trenches instead of sandbags. President Wilson's pushing America into the war will only strengthen the czar's resolve. A weakened czar—a defeated czar—will lead to him being thrown out on his ass, creating a vacuum. Revolutionary defeatism, that's the ticket! Comrade Lenin's Bolsheviks will fill this vacuum. That, in my not-so-humble opinion, is what we must work for. Those of us who, like you, have a voice must bend all our efforts to keep America out of the war and Russia in the war."

I sipped at my beer, trying to digest Gregory's pessimism. "I concede you know America better than I do," I eventually managed. "Still, correct me if I'm wrong but Americans made revolution once, and their example ignited a fuse leading to revolution in France. I live with the expectation—the hope!—that the New World can again show the Greek goddess Europa the way forward to egalitarian societies."

"I admired you in 1905, Trotsky," Gregory sniffed. "I still admire you in 1917. Dream on."

7

Give women the vote, one might run for president . . .

I REGRET TO REPORT THAT, with one notable exception, Bukharin's great Socialist pals in Brooklyn were neither great nor seriously Socialist nor pals.

With Aleksandra Kollontai, her hair a tangled nest of unwashed curls, leading the way to the sprawling no-man's-land on the other side of the East River where sightseers rarely set foot—thanks to her son, Misha, who worked in a capitalist automobile factory in the New Jersey, she had mastered New York's labyrinthian metro system—the three of us inserted our buffalo nickels in the turnstiles and headed east on the Interborough Rapid Transit over the Brooklyn Bridge. As there was still a shard of daylight, I caught a glimpse of machine guns set up behind sandbags at the base of the bridge's towers; clearly America was prepping to enter the Great War raging in Europe. Bukharin, who was drawn to anything clandestine, had organized what he called a "secret dinner" with the leading icons of American

Socialism. Hanging on to overhead straps for dear life, we were so deep in conversation that we almost missed our Fifty-Fourth Street stop. Aleksandra used one of her ankle-length lace-ups to stop the door from shutting and, giggling like schoolchildren, we escaped into the Borough Park station.

Bukharin's secret dinner turned out to be in the smoke-filled flat of Ludwig Lore, the overheavy, sharp-tongued German-born editor of the *New Yorker Volkszeitung*, where I had already published several freelance articles. (I spotted yellowish soup stains on his red-and-white striped cravat, advertisements, so I presumed, for his working-class roots and instincts.) Lore's wife, who was never introduced so I took her for a maid until she joined us at the table, was baking muffins in a minuscule kitchen when we arrived. I knew the Russians in the room personally, starting with Gregory Weinstein, my editor at *Novy Mir*. The non-Russians were new to me. I never did catch all their names but I recognized two of them by reputation: Morris Hillquit, the founder of the American Socialist Party (Aleksandra despised Hillquit, whispering to me that he was a vile revisionist who didn't have the guts to organize a serious strike, forget revolution); and the Socialist star Eugene Debs, hero of legendary Chicago Pullman strike who ran for president four times on the Socialist ticket. (Needless to say, he came in last four times.) As for the notable exception I mentioned—are you sitting down?—he was that rarest of birds, a young American Communist, whom I took a liking to at first sight. His name was Lou Fraina. He made a living editing the magazine *Modern Dance*, of all things, but he dreamed of founding an American Communist Party to fan the flame of revolution, not ballet.

Litzky had warned me to keep my impatience under wraps. *Keep in mind the old Russian adage: Quieter than water, shorter than grass. That's you tonight, got it, Bronshtein?*

Got it, I agreed reluctantly.

"We are in a life-and-death struggle," Hillquit was saying, while around him balding heads nodded in grim agreement, "'gainst them that aim to oblige workers to work longer hours for miserable salaries."

"That there explains why the notorious agent of the ruling class Thomas Edison invented the light bulb," one of the non-Russians, a young man who, like me, wore a pince-nez on the bridge of his nose, said. "It was a capitalist plot to keep the noses of workers glued to the grindstone." He looked around the table for support; finding none, he doubled down. "Lookit, it ain't Jules Verne rocket science—if Henry Ford can light up the night, he can keep his Ford Ts rolling off one of his newfangled assembly lines until the wee hours of the morning."

"The answer to Mr. Edison's light bulb is revolution," I interjected. Twelve heads swiveled in my direction to stare at the Martian in their midst.

Quieter than water, Litzky spit into my ear. *Remember?*

But all was not lost. That rarest of birds, the American

Communist Lou Fraina, came round the table to offer me a plate of Mrs. Lore's muffins. "Mr. Trotsky here has something in common with the nocturnal bat: Night vision," he said. "Even in the dark he can see past your capitalist clichés to identify the nub of the problem. We are not going to change things by turning off the lights in factories at sunset. We are going to change things when the workers own those factories—"

"When the proletariat owns the means of production," I put in. I leaned over Mrs. Lore's muffins. "Imagine extraterrestrials landing on planet earth and trying to figure out why czars and kings rule Russia and England while workers slaving away in death traps we call factories are forced to settle for the crumbs that fall from the capitalists' tables."

The stifled rumbling from the far end of the table sounded suspiciously like the faint forewarning that comes before an earthquake. "Hellfire," Debs blurted out, "if we can cut into the profits of capitalist bloodsuckers living off the surplus value workers produce by turning off the goddanged lights—by shutting down the goddanged electricity—at sunset, Trotsky, we could move on to the next item on our agenda."

"Could I trouble you to identify the next item," I said politely.

"A minimum living wage, Trotsky," he snarled. "How much cash workers find in their pay packets at the end of the six-day workweek."

"Health care," someone sitting on a radiator added.

"How about on-the-job accident insurance."

"Guaranteeing the right to strike, arresting strikebreakers hired by the bosses."

"Factory and mine inspection laws."

"Don't forget child labor laws, for heaven's sake."

"And while we're at it, why not paid vacations?"

"Why the hell not?" the non-Russian with the pince-nez agreed.

"You gentlemen are all forgetting maternity leave," Mrs. Lore declared. She glanced around, a bit startled to have heard her own voice join the conversation.

"Maternity leave is on the agenda, my dear," her husband, Ludwig Lore, ironing his unruly black mustache with an index finger, told her, "just far down."

"Figures," Aleksandra Kollontai muttered.

"Did you say something?" Hillquit inquired.

Aleksandra, whom her Bolshevik comrades knew to be a freethinking female when it came to defining a woman's role in society, quitting a husband and flaunting a drove of lovers over the years to prove it, leapt to her feet. "I did, actually. I said that it's not surprising maternity leave is at the bottom of your Socialist agenda in a country where women still don't have the right to vote."

"We Socialists are obliged to pick our fights," Debs grumbled. "Americans aren't ready to give women, who spend most of their waking hours in the goddanged kitchen, a say in the election of presidents and senators and governors."

"Give women the vote," the non-Russian with the pince-nez exclaimed, "next thing you know one of them might take it into her pretty head to run for president."

Aleksandra, no wallflower, rose to the occasion. "After your revolution against Great Britain and its demented king, George with a Roman numeral three after his name," she said, a deceptively innocent smile playing on her lovely lips, "you reckoned that a person of color counted for three-fifths of a white male when it came to apportioning seats in your House of Representatives. Now you're relegating the female, half of the hundred million people living in America, to three-fifths of a male."

"I thought you said she was a Bolshevik," another of the non-Russians complained to Ludwig Lore, "not one of those insufferable suffragettes."

"I am all three," Aleksandra said with a lethal smile. "A Bolshevik and a suffragette and insufferable."

Bukharin, at the other end of the table, rapped his knife against a glass in approval. I chimed in. "When we Bolsheviks oust the czar and take power in Russia, women will certainly get the right to vote."

Ludwig Lore melted back into his chair, his potbelly coming into view as he eyed me across the table. "How long have you been in these United States of America, Mr. Trotsky?" he inquired.

"Funny thing, that fella Hoover from the Bureau of Investigation told me that Americans were happy with

America as it is," I remarked. "I suppose that includes the Americans who call themselves Socialists. To answer your question, Mr. Lore: Marx himself never lived in America but his insights—you've all read Karl Marx I presume—can offer solutions to industrialization, to exploitation, to surplus value, to alienation. A state run by the working class, where women abandon their kitchens in order to work as well as to vote, will do away with private property—the workers will own the property and share the wealth it produces."

For once my conscience Litzky seemed pleased with me. *Hurrah, Bronshtein. Another applecart upended!*

Debs tugged at the cloth napkin tucked under his starched collar and folded it carefully on the table. "I understand that you are a latecomer to the English language, Trotsky. Are you sure you know what you're saying? Are you sure you're not auditioning for one of those goddanged Hollywood picture shows?"

"I can repeat what I said in Russian or German or French if it will convince you I know what I am saying when I speak English." I'm afraid I couldn't resist adding, "*Kotu na smekh*—it's enough to make a cat laugh. Joining your American Socialist Party is like drinking what the working class calls near beer, the weak non-alcoholic swill that we feed to our pigs in Ukraine."

I caught the unmistakable sound of Litzky moaning.

Morris Hillquit scraped back his chair and stood up. "He's dreaming," he said. "You're dreaming, Mr. Trotsky. Good grief, come back down to earth. The Chinese have a saying: A journey of a thousand miles begins with a single step. That single first step is a living wage and shorter hours in the sweat shops." He turned to the others around the table. "I suspect we're wasting our breath talking to a Bolshevik who thinks revolution is the answer to all our problems."

So much for Leon Trotsky lighting the fuse to world revolution in America, Litzky taunted me.

I haven't shot the last arrow in my quiver, I assured my conscience.

"Your muffins were delicious," I told Mrs. Lore at the door. "Thank you for your hospitality."

She seemed at a loss for words. "I guess," she mumbled.

8

They regret you came, they'll celebrate when you leave . . .

IF I CAN HONESTLY SAY that Bukharin's secret meeting in Brooklyn didn't go well—I didn't esteem most of these putative Socialists he and Aleksandra Kollontai had rounded up, and they obviously didn't esteem yours truly—the post-mortem with my better angel Litzky went worse. *Bronshtein, Bronshtein, you who have been beaten to a pulp by the czar's police and condemned to the tender mercies of Siberia, you who have seen with your own tear-shot eyes Albanian bodies rotting in Balkan cornfields, your naivety at the overripe age of thirty-eight—your excruciating unworldliness!—drives me up the goddamn wall. These are American Socialists, Bronshtein, which means they are hybrid capitalists who spend their waking hours trying to figure out how to get a bigger slice of the pie. Period.*

You are too cynical to be a practicing conscience, I snapped, a bit surprised by the belligerent edge to the voice in my brain that I recognized as mine. Like Paul on the road to Damascus, I heard myself lecturing my conscience, your

American Socialists are ripe for revelation. The words were barely in the air between us when I caught what sounded like Litzky's distinctive snort, which was his usual reaction when I had the gall to disagree with him. *Road to Damascus! What are you, a freaking travel agent? Despite what you discovered at Bukharin's secret dinner, don't tell me you still see yourself supplying the revelation that rouses American Socialists to revolution!*

If not me, who? I demanded.

This appeared to disconcert my conscience. *Did I hear what I think I heard: Lev atheist-to-the-marrow Bronshtein quoting Hillel the Elder! You need to make up your goddamn mind, Bronshtein—are you a disciple of the Bolshevik Lenin or the patriarch Moses or the Jew Jesus?*

I was beginning to take perverse pleasure in the verbal jousting with my conscience. Not for the first time, I shot back, you simplify complex things: Even American Socialism—especially American Socialism—contains within it the seed of revolution. Having been raised on my father's farm, I know something about seeds, I added. They need to be nurtured, they need to be coddled, they need to be watered—

I didn't get to finish the thought. *My pathetic misguided Bronshtein, seed or no seed, revolution in the United States of North America is the next to last thing on their list, right below poor Mrs. Lore's maternity leave.*

And what, in your opinion, is the last thing? I demanded.

I could hear my conscience almost choking on a laugh. *Comrade Trotsky is the last thing, my dear Bronshtein. They regret you came, they'll celebrate when you leave, they couldn't care less that the great Trotsky who chaired the first soviet during the 1905 Russian revolution has honored them with his presence in these United States of North America.*

I heard Nata calling me from the bedroom. "Do you know what time it is, Lev? Come to sleep, for pity's sake."

"I'm too exhausted to sleep," I called back.

"Tomorrow's another day," I heard her say.

"Are you absolutely sure?" I asked.

9

You won't survive the revolution you make . . .

I'LL TAKE A WILD GUESS: Woodrow Wilson, who ran for president on the slogan "He kept us out of war," wasn't reading my columns in *Novy Mir* (or my freelance articles in the *Jewish Daily Forward* or the *New Yorker Volkszeitung*, for that matter). Or if he was reading them, he wasn't persuaded by the peacemongering of a Russian living in exile in the Bronx. At the end of January, with the Germans having resumed unrestricted submarine warfare (one U-boat sank the British steamer *Eavestone* and then opened fire on the lifeboat, killing the ship's captain and three passengers), Wilson broke off diplomatic relations with Berlin. "Who will profit?" I screamed in print, rolling my editorial boulder up the steep hill of American hubris in a desperate attempt to head off what was beginning to seem inevitable. "Global capitalism will profit! Who will bleed? The workers of the world will do the bleeding! Never forget, in this spasm of supposed patriotism, that there are workers on both ends of the bayonet."

Litzky tried to console me. *You are a voice crying in the wilderness, Bronshtein*, he murmured in my ear.

If I can't quote Hillel the Elder, I retorted, you need to stop trying to comfort me with quotations from the Christian Bible.

With or without the comfort of a conscience, there was no escaping the fact that war fever was raging in America. The straw that broke this camel's back was an editorial in the supposedly Socialist *Jewish Daily Forward* supporting American entry into the war. Barely able to believe my eyes, I dropped what I was doing and made my way to the *Forward*'s sanctum, a ten-story edifice on East Broadway facing Seward Park with its bas-relief portraits of Marx and Engels on one outside wall (frowning in disagreement with the *Forward*'s warmongering, so I imagined). I had run across Abraham Cahan, the *Forward*'s cantankerous editor in chief and founder, at a conference Bukharin had organized. "I'm sorry, Mr. Trotsky, but Mr. Cahan is in a meeting," a secretary with short bobbed blond hair informed me—but I was in no mood to be put off. I barged into his lion's den, with the secretary in high heels hard on my low heels. "I couldn't stop him, Mr. Cahan," she cried. Cahan, some twenty years my senior, was standing in front of an ornate mirror trimming his bushy mustache with a tiny pair of scissors. He wagged a finger and the secretary, favoring me with a nasty look, retreated, closing the door behind her. "To what do I owe this intrusion, Mr. Trotsky?" Cahan demanded, settling his Socialist rump onto the leather swivel chair behind his enormous desk.

"You owe this intrusion, Mr. Cahan, to my expectation that you will be persuaded to reconsider the *Forward*'s editorial policy supporting American entry into the war."

"How long have you been in America, Mr. Trotsky?"

"Why is it everyone hits me over the head with this question?" I shot back, but he wasn't to be put off.

"All of three weeks, I calculate," Cahan said.

"It's closer to four," I corrected him.

"Three, four, and you really think you know more about American foreign policy than those of us who have lived here a lifetime? What arrogance!"

In an instant, our dialogue turned into a shrill shouting match. "Socialist patriot," I yelled.

"Bolshevik apostate," he bellowed back.

"You talk a good Socialist game," I hollered, "but when push comes to shove, you fall in line behind the jingoistic flag-wavers."

"Fuck you, Trotsky!"

"Fuck me," I agreed.

I heard Litzky's sarcastic drawl in my ear. *So much for your publishing freelance articles in Cahan's Yiddish rag.*

"Talk about burning bridges," Nata said when I recounted my confrontation with Cahan to her later that day. "The fifteen dollars he paid you for an article came in handy. Both the boys need new knickerbockers, not to mention haircuts and lunch money at the public schools where I enrolled them."

"He needed correction," I said, stubbornly defending myself.

"You, our breadwinner, need discretion," Nata shot back.

Litzky, as usual, couldn't resist putting in his two cents. *She's not wrong*, he whispered in my ear.

She's right from her point of view, I instructed my conscience, but her point of view is wrong.

"You're talking to whom?" Nata inquired innocently—as if she didn't know.

"I'm talking to my nombril."

The confrontation with Cahan, which capped an already difficult day at the office, had left my irritability on a short fuse. Back at the *Novy Mir* basement office the next morning, I composed a scathing column about the treachery of pretend Socialists who tow the capitalist line to sell newspapers. I was dotting the i's and crossing the t's when Aleksandra Kollontai, Lenin's eyes and ears in New York, came over with a letter from someone pretending to be my French literary agent. "I don't have a French literary agent," I told her.

Aleksandra produced a furtive smile. "Light a candle," she ordered.

"Ahhh, it's that kind of letter," I said. I retrieved a candle from a desk drawer and, igniting the wick, held the paper over the flame to develop the hidden writing. Small yellowish letters gradually materialized between the inked lines. It turned out to be a secret letter from none other than Vladimir Lenin. "First order of business when we Bolsheviks seize power in Russia, colon," I read aloud. "Reform Russian alphabet, simplify spelling. This, more than arcane economic restructuring that puts means of production into the hands of the relatively few urban proletarians, will attract hordes of illiterate peasants to our cause."

Aleksandra inquired sweetly, "Do I have your permission, Comrade Trotsky, to inform Vladimir Ilyich that you are on board?"

"For the revolution or simplifying spelling?" I quipped.

"Either, or," she said. "Ideally, both."

Pinned to the wall by Aleksandra's teasing smile, my irritability dissipated. "Yes, yes. He can count on me. Someone who thinks that simplifying spelling can save Mother Russia can't be nearly as dangerous as his enemies claim." I leaned across my desk and asked in an undertone, "How is it you know about candles and secret writing?"

She glanced over her shoulder to be sure no one at *Novy Mir* was within earshot. "When I first became involved with the Marxist radicals in Saint Petersburg, I was the comrade charged with organizing communications between Lenin and his friends in exile abroad, you among them. By what—as long as you didn't look too closely—appeared to be a coincidence, my companion at the time just happened to be the Okhrana investigator who'd been assigned the Bolshevik dossier. To answer your question, it was my lover who initiated me into the fine art of codes and secret writing."

"You're making this up," I decided.

She had to laugh. "Maybe I am, then again maybe I'm not." Aleksandra obviously got a charge out of playing Mata Hari, the notorious German spy who'd been arrested in France, and would have elaborated on the role if we hadn't been distracted by the tinkling of the bell above the front door. And in she walked, she being the half Mexican, half Jewish, half journalist from the *Brooklyn Daily Eagle* who had shouted questions at me on the pier the day I set foot in America. "Remember me, Mr. Trotsky?" she called now as she limped across the room, her cuffed corduroy trousers scraping the sawdust on the floor, and came to a full stop in front of my desk. "Foot fell asleep on the trolleybus," she said, explaining the limp. "Still waking up. Hey, name's Fred Fédora."

"You don't look much like a Fred," I teased.

Bukharin, monitoring the conversation from the next desk, and Aleksandra, who'd gone over to stir the cabbage soup cooking on one of the tabletop gas burners, seemed amused.

"Fred," Fred explained, undoubtedly for the thousandth time, "is short for Frederika, but as my progenitor had his heart set on a son, Fred got itself stuck to my female body." She dropped a folded copy of that morning's *Eagle* on my desk and I read one headline aloud: "SPEED WORK ON NET TO PROTECT HARBOR AGAINST SUBMARINES."

"Seems as if America is getting ready to join the war," Bukharin said.

"Looks that way," I agreed.

"Hey," Fred said, "I hear on my grapevine you had a knock-down, drag-out donnybrook with Cahan over at the *Forward*. I'd like to write a piece about your squabble."

"As you can see, I'm pretty busy," I told her.

"Come on, Mr. Trotsky, don't be a wet blanket. If I can get an exclusive with the cat's meow, it would make my day. Not to mention help my newshawk's career."

"Didn't know," Bukharin remarked in Russian from the next desk, "you had something in common with the meow of a cat."

I sat back and inspected her. She was fetching in a disheveled sort of way: Untamed eyebrows, short brown hair that looked as if it had been hacked as opposed to trimmed and tickled the back of her long neck, lips and fingernails painted the same shade of fire-engine red, the absence of an undergarment if the nipples pushing into her soft V-neck sweater could be trusted. A large silver hoop dangling from one earlobe caught shards of sunlight when she turned her head. "Grapevine, donnybrook, wet blanket, cat's meow," I said. "Kindly tell me what language you're speaking?"

Fred grinned—and it was the tight-lipped grin, which tainted her eyes and made her appear to be taunting the person on the receiving end of the grin, that seduced me. "I'd say the King's English if I wasn't standing here in Greenwich

Village, North America," she said. "Please, Mr. Trotsky, I'm just a biscuit looking for a scoop from someone who knows his onions."

I exchanged looks with Bukharin, who seemed charmed by the girl's impudence, if not her slang-mangled jargon.

"So," she said, "I take it you are dead set against the whole kaboodle—"

"Kaboodle?"

"—of America plunging into this war with Germany," she went on.

I began to see the advantage of agreeing to an interview: My reasons for opposing America joining in the European war would find a larger audience. "I'd offer you a chair if I had a chair to offer," I said.

She looked around, startled to discover that journalism at *Novy Mir* had come to a grinding halt: The linotype had ceased spitting out molten slugs of Gothic font; Gregory Weinstein, a bib around his wrinkled neck and munching on a frankfurter roll chock-full of sauerkraut, had stopped chewing; even the Western Union messenger in knee boots delivering the morning's batch of telegrams stood next to the secretary's desk like a frozen motion picture frame. All nine people present in *Novy Mir*'s cabbage-scented basement office appeared to be hanging on Fred's every word. "The Monopole over on Second Avenue might be a more congenial place to jaw," she suggested quietly. "What would you say to a stein of tap beer and a steak sandwich, Mr.

Trotsky?" And that contagious grin of hers swept all before it like a groundswell washing debris from a beach. "Hey, the *Brooklyn Daily Eagle* will pick up the tab if you sit still for an interview."

Which is how I wound up next to Fred on one of the Monopole's leather-bound benches, relishing that American contribution to gastronomic excellence, a steak sandwich, and, between bites, mumbling answers to her questions as she scribbled indecipherable notes in a pad. We had covered my little spat with Cahan over the *Forward*'s disgraceful editorial and moved on to what really interested her: My take on revolution in Russia. "You're barking up the wrong tree," she said at one point. "My daddy, who decided I was a Fred and raised me to think like one, was your intellectual twin: The more he read about the nineteenth-century industrial revolution that transformed agrarian societies into urban craters, the more he was convinced that mass mutiny was the answer. Trouble was he claimed to know the answer before he had time to mull the question. Okay, blood spilled in revolution has the salving grace of wiping the slate clean. But what comes after, that's the sixty-four dollar question my father never wrestled with, Mr. Trotsky."

I reached under the table and carelessly slipped my hand onto her knee. "Please call me Leo."

I couldn't miss Litzky's nervous cough in my mind's ear. *Bronshtein!* was all he said, his voice rising on the second syllable.

Fred glanced down at my hand but didn't try to dislodge it. "You're married, aren't you, Mr. . . . Leo?"

"I am. This is off the record, right? The lady Mr. Hoover from your Bureau of Investigation called my lawful wedded wife is trapped in Siberia with my two daughters. Natalya, the woman who came to America with me, has been my companion for years. She is the mother of my two sons, which, to my mind, is a stronger bond than marriage."

"How did you and Natalya meet?"

Give her the expurgated version, for Pete's sake, Litzky warned, *lest you shock the knickers off her.*

"It was in Odessa," I said, savoring my conscience's discomfort, "at one of those interminable Socialist conferences. As Nata had done time in one of the czar's prisons—for attending an illegal May Day proletariat rally in Saint Petersburg—she was invited to sit next to me on the stage. And I happened to notice she was wearing one of those newfangled German brassieres. Afterward eight or ten of us were drinking ersatz coffee in the worker's canteen—and when she leaned over to reach for the sugar cellar I couldn't help but see she was not wearing the brassiere."

"Lust at first sight! And then what happened?"

"I asked her if we could have a drink at the canteen's private bar in order to see if we could have supper together in order to see if we would sleep together that night in order to see if a journey of a thousand nights could begin with a one-night stand."

"And of course she agreed?"

"Of course she refused! She was, by then, what came to be called a feminist, which is to say a female of the species liberated from the shackles of bourgeois relationships, but she didn't appreciate being swept off her feet. Still, I could tell she was charmed by my bluntness. And as I wouldn't take no for an answer, my persistence paid off when she finally agreed to have a single drink with me." I had to smile at the memory. "Naturally one thing led to another. The first chance I got—we were in the darkened attic of friends of hers looking at their newborn kittens—I reached under Nata's blouse and put a hand on her breast. That led to a memorable one-night stand. Some months later, when our paths happened to cross again in Saint Petersburg, we took the relationship to the next level. The rest is history."

You couldn't resist, could you, Bronshtein!

I stared pointedly at Fred's left hand, which was wrapped around her sweating stein of tap beer. "You wear a wedding band . . ."

She folded her notepad and slipped it into her leather shoulder sack. "I happen to be married to a City College professor of literature, of all things, but I absolutely refuse to be condemned to lifelong fidelity because I made the mistake of marrying the first man who put his penis in my mouth."

Oy vey, Litzky gasped into my mind's ear. *You went hog so she felt obligated to go whole hog!*

Suddenly, frighteningly, I could make out Fred's muffled

voice droning on. "Neither of us believes . . . confusing marriage with prison . . . works as long as you're both open to casual sex . . ."

Fred was explaining things that I didn't want explained. How for God's sake can a marriage be open? Open to what? How can sex be casual? To add to my bewilderment my pince-nez fogged up. I jerked it off the bridge of my nose and began desperately cleaning the lenses on my tie when I felt Litzky's sizzling breath roasting the lobe of my ear. *You need to watch your ass, Bronshtein. Your brain is what's fogged up, not your eyeglasses. If you were able to think straight you would see you're standing on the high bank of the swollen river the Greeks called Styx.*

Ignoring Litzky's forebodings, I plunged headfirst into his turbulent Styx: "I've never met anybody quite like you," I gushed. And my fingers lingering on Fred's knee migrated north—of their own accord, mind you, I swear on the heads of my boys I didn't know where they were going until my perspiring palm came to rest on the inside of her thigh.

"You all right, Leo?" She favored me with one of her tantalizing grins and, discovering that she was speaking words I actually understood, I managed to slow my racing pulse down to a fast jog. "Hey, consider the probability," she said with a laugh in her throat, "that you never met anyone like me because they broke the mold after I was incarnated."

I racked my brain for a comfortable buoy that I could

cling to to keep from drowning in mortification. "The sixty-four dollar question your father never wrestled with—"

"Yes, yes. Please go on, Leo. I'm fascinated to hear a world-famous revolutionist explain what happens after the workers mutiny."

I took it as a reprieve to be back on the rock-solid ground of Marxist theory. "What happens, my dear Fred, is we will create a classless society that will put an end to poverty, to exploitation by landlords and factory foremen and filthy rich estate owners, to anti-Semitism and bigotry in all its guises and disguises. The Marxist formulation 'From each according to his ability, to each according to his needs' will even put an end to crime, since with free access to goods and services there will be no need to steal." I permitted my fingers to drift higher on her thigh. "And that's only the beginning: I learned today that one of the first things Comrade Lenin plans to do after taking power is reform the Russian alphabet, which will simplify spelling for dozens of millions of semiliterate peasants."

"Will he simplify spelling before or after he puts an end to anti-Semitism?" she asked with a straight face.

"You're treating this as if it were a joke. We're serious people proposing to do serious things."

"You're right to be annoyed," Fred allowed, lightly fondling with her fire-engine red fingertips the back of my hand stuck to her thigh. She took a swig of beer and rolled it around in her mouth, as if she were using it to clean her teeth, before swallowing. "Okay, here's a serious question for a serious Russian revolutionist: Do you Bolsheviks believe in equality at the starting block or the finish line? Bleeding-heart liberals like me are all for equality at the starting block, but we take into account that some people simply run faster than others—we're not all blessed with the same amount of talent, the same amount of ambition, the same amount of energy in our legs."

Being a veteran of Lenin's Zurich *kaffeeklatsch* and its ersatz coffee, I felt as if I were swimming in unruffled water as opposed to Litzky's raging Styx. "The rat race in a capitalist environment is rigged, Fred—it's all about who you know, it's all about how rich your parents are and what education, given their wealth, you had access to. It's about the color of your skin, for God's sake. No, no, I believe—Lenin's Bolsheviks believe—that, in a Socialist environment, equality at the starting block must lead to equality at the finish line. What's the point of revolution if it doesn't?" I tightened my grip on her thigh to emphasize my words. "Who knows—equality at the finish line could even benefit the feminine sex. It's only global equality that can bring about a worker's utopia for men and women alike, as well as the withering away of the state and its oppressive organs."

Fred snickered. "Come clean, huh, Leo? You don't really expect the state to wither away, do you? Hey, if you wind up running the show, I guarantee you'll change your tune. The last thing you'll do if you're the state is wither away."

"How come you're familiar with concepts like the withering away of the state?"

"I was a Marxist before I wasn't a Marxist."

"Why did you stop being a Marxist?"

"I suppose it was when I figured out it didn't matter if the workers owned the factories when what the factories produced was killing us anyhow."

She's running rings around you, Bronshtein. Educate her, for Pete's sake—explain that the withering away of the state is a long-term goal.

"The withering away of the state is a long-term goal," I informed her.

Fred laughed under her breath. "I'll bet it's a very loooooong-term goal! Hey, don't get me wrong—I think you're heroic to propose revolution in Russia, or in America for that matter. Especially as it's a historical given that revolutions devour their children. Which means there is a strong possibility you won't survive the revolution you make." She waved a hand to discourage me from discouraging her. "I speak from bitter experience when I say revolutions devour their children, Leo. My father, his name was Mateo, was one of the peasants with Emiliano Zapata in Morelos when they launched what you call revolution and I think of as mass mutiny, first against Francisco Madero, then, after he was murdered, against his assassin, Victoriano Huerta. That was four years ago, in 1913. My sister and I, at my father's urging, had already escaped to North America, which is how

I wound up in the boondock called Brooklyn. How well do you know Mexican history? Zapata's peasant army, fighting for agrarian reforms, was routing the federales when, one fine day, they put my father up against the side of a barn and shot him dead because he wouldn't go along with hanging the big landowners. If your Vladimir Lenin succeeds in making revolution in Russia, trust me, he will be every bit as ruthless as Emiliano Zapata, who hanged landowners and murdered my father."

I started to shake my head. "I think you misread history—"

But she interrupted my interruption with a quote from the horse's mouth that we were both familiar with: "'Enemies of a workers' state,' your Lenin famously said, 'must be shortened by a head.'" Fred's taunting grin materialized on her lips. "Shortened by a head," she repeated as if it were the refrain of a song she had sung. "Nice, huh?"

"There are respectable historians," I remarked, "who think the French Revolution owed its success to Monsieur Guillotin's contraption that made its enemies shorter by a head."

"If you swallow that, it puts you in the same boat as your Vladimir Lenin," she said dryly.

"I'd consider it an honor to share a boat with Vladimir Lenin," I shot back, but I wasn't sure Fred was still following the conversation. She was peering at the minuscule watch strapped to her delicate wrist.

"Oh Christ, I didn't realize the time! To be continued."

She brought her knees together, trapping my hand on her thigh. "What are you doing this afternoon, Leo?"

Resist temptation, Bronshtein, if you are still in charge of your penis, as opposed to vice versa, Litzky warned.

I took a deep breath. "My column for tomorrow's paper is already set in type, so I'm free as a bird," I told her. "This afternoon I'm doing whatever you're doing."

"Come on then, fly with me—I'll introduce you to your doppelgänger, the jubilant revolutionist Charlie Chaplin."

10

Do you or don't you want to get your ashes hauled . . .

I KNEW THE WORLD WAS awash with Socialist doppelgängers (Karl Marx wouldn't have invited the workers of the world to unite if there weren't hordes of them out there chafing at the capitalist bit), but the last thing I expected was to come face-to-face with one in a murky Broadway movie theater. The preview of the silent film Fred took me to see, it was called *The Immigrant*, had only just opened, but word of mouth had preceded it and the line at the box office stretched down the block and around the corner. Luckily for us, being a working journalist Fred pretended that she was reviewing the film and, flashing her press card, she was waved through with me in tow. From the moment the house lights dimmed and the black-and-white images began to flicker on the silver screen, I was startled by the lump in my throat. The tramp steamer transporting immigrants to America in the opening sequence, with its two stacks belching tongues of black smoke as the bow plowed through

Atlantic swells, was the spitting image of the *Montserrat*, the ship I'd come over on, and—please don't laugh—I swear I felt the theater's wooden floor planks rising and sinking under the soles of my shoes. In one of the first scenes, my doppelgänger, this Englishman Chaplin who was making a name for himself on the silver screen, could be seen bent over the railing as the ship pitched through high seas. It looked as if he, like my son Sergei on the *Montserrat*, was seasick and throwing up—until Chaplin straightened and we saw he'd been fishing, my God, saw he had even caught a fish. I felt an instant kinship with this Charlie Chaplin fellow, with a one-size-too-small bowler glued to his scalp and an incongruous toothbrush mustache fixed on his upper lip, as he gazed at Lady Liberty drifting past. (I'll wager that he, like me, noticed that her back was turned to America.) Watching Chaplin's penniless immigrant disembarking in New York, I saw myself arriving in the New World all over again—the only thing missing from Mr. Chaplin's tribulations was your Mr. Hoover and his Bureau of Investigation giving him a hard time before stamping his passport.

Even the silent film's piano player appeared to be mesmerized by the images flickering on the screen: Sitting in the theater's twilight under the stage, a cigarette dangling from his mouth, he kept his eyes fixed on the screen above his head as he filled the hall with ripples of music that echoed the mood of the Little Tramp.

"I can see you like the film," Fred whispered, the tips of

her fingers resting lightly on the back of my hand camped on her thigh.

"I'm beginning to understand why you think of this Chaplin as my doppelgänger," I whispered back. Litzky had been uncommonly quiet, but I suddenly heard his nasal growl in my mind's ear. *He is definitely Communistically inclined*, my conscience decided. *You only have to look in his eyes to see where his heart is.*

As if on cue, Chaplin's tramp reared back and with one of his king-size shoes kicked a customs officer in the backside. The audience, me among them, roared in delight. "Revolutions begin," I told Fred, "with the first downtrodden proletarian inflicting punishment that fits the capitalist crime."

This Chaplin fellow had worked his magic on me and I was still enthralled when we emerged from the theater. On the sidewalk, light from Mr. Edison's yellow arc lamps and giant billboards, including the gaudy Ziegfeld advertisement that Nata considered vulgar, was beginning to gouge the Manhattan dusk. Broadway itself was choked with horse-drawn carriages and delivery wagons. At the intersection with Forty-Second Street, an overweight policeman stood in the middle of traffic waving his arms and blowing on a shrill whistle that nobody seemed to pay attention to. The occasional automobile, its klaxon madly hooting at the slower vehicles, already had its headlamps on.

"So do you or don't you?" Fred demanded.

"Do I what?"

"Do you or don't you want to get your ashes hauled?"

"Ashes—hauled?"

"Do you want to shack up?"

"Shack—up?"

"Do you want to get laid, for Christ's sake?"

I planted myself in front of Fred. "There you go again, speaking that foreign language of yours. But your tone, not to mention the glint in your eye, offers clues to a Russian newly come to the King's English: Does your *ashes hauled*, your *shack up*, your *get laid* mean what I think it means? Are you proposing to have sexual intercourse with me?"

Fred was savoring my discomfort. "For someone who spent half the afternoon with his hand on my thigh, your ignorance is far-fetched. Everyone knows you're Jewish, which means you're circumcised. I have a weakness for circumcised. So, hey, I'm as horny as you are."

"Horny?"

"I want sex as much as you do."

Flustered, all I could think to say was, "You don't beat about the bush."

Grinning that grin she owned the patent to, she said, "'Bush' happens to be slang for female pubic hair—I reckon a notorious revolutionist like you might enjoy beating about my bush."

Out of the frying pan into the fire, Litzky muttered with his distinctive sneer.

Fire was an accurate metaphor for what transpired in the seedy hotel on a side street off Broadway where rooms rented by the hour, payment up front, only cash was accepted, clean sheets were available for $1 extra. Priding herself on being a free-thinking female and, as I later discovered, a card-carrying member of the Brooklyn Heights suffragettes, Fred insisted on paying half the bill, which turned out to be $7 including a half bottle of cheap white wine. Given the dismal state of my finances, I was in no position to refuse. The room, a third-floor walkup at the end of a dingy corridor that reeked of urine, was only slightly larger than the four-poster bed fitted with a mattress that sagged like a hammock under the weight of our unclothed bodies. A beeswax-yellow neon sign across the street must have short-circuited because it kept blinking on and off, and for a split second I imagined it was sending a cease-and-desist message from Litzky in Morse code. I would have pulled down the window shade if there had been a window shade. It must have been our second hour in the room before I tuned back in to spoken speech. "Where did you learn to do that?" I gasped.

Fred came up for air. "It's not something that's taught, for Christ's sake, so it's not something you learn." She crept up alongside me and with her lips against my ear whispered, "You make love like an intellectual, Leo."

Normally I don't object to being called an intellectual, but wedged in the hammock of a bed I didn't take her remark as a compliment. "How, pray tell, does an intellectual make love?" I inquired.

"You get your pleasure from your brain instead of your body. A little voice in your brain tells you, 'Wow, look at me—I'm actually getting laid so this has to be exciting.'" (*She's got your number, Bronshtein!* Litzky warned me in my mind's ear.) Fred suddenly propped herself up on an elbow. "What is the Russian attitude toward reciprocity?"

"Reciprocity?" I repeated in confusion.

She spelled it out. "Do unto others as you would have others do unto you."

The penny dropped. "Ahhh," I said, and I did unto her what she had done unto me. "I really enjoyed that," I rasped when it was my turn to come up for air.

"You sound surprised," she said. "Me, also, I enjoyed that," she confessed in a voice I didn't recognize. Then she added, "I hope this meeting of minds and bodies has a sequel."

In for a penny, in for a pound, Litzky declared, his caustic singsong voice ringing in my mind's ear. Do me a favor and fuck off, I sneered.

"Did I hear you right, Leo?" Fred demanded. "You want to fuck again! Hey, maybe you're not a repressed intellectual after all!"

11

You've turned into a vulgar American in America . . .

THE BOYS WERE ALREADY IN their bunk beds, Sergei's nine-year-old eyelids twitching with fatigue, Lyova reading *The Adventures of Paddy the Beaver* by candlelight to improve his English. I settled onto the edge of Lyova's bed. "Tell me, boys, what animal would you have liked to be if you could have been born an animal?"

"That's easy, father," Sergei said. "A vulture."

"And why a vulture?"

"I should very much like to soar high above the world and, drifting on gusts of wind, see it from a great height. And when I'm hungry I'll dive down and snare a fat mouse in a field that has just been plowed and is crawling with mice."

"If I understand you correctly, you draw the line at eating worms but you're okay with mice?"

Sergei blushed in embarrassment. "It's only make-believe, father."

"And you, Lyova? Which animal would you like to be?"

"A spider, father. They are wonderful architects. I enjoy watching them weave their webs with fine silk threads that look delicate but can withstand torrents of wind and rain. I am fascinated by the spider's patience, waiting as they do for some unsuspecting fly to stray into their web, at which point they bind the fly with silk threads and dine on it for days and days."

"What about you, father?" Sergei asked. "What animal would you have liked to be?"

"Ha! I have already been reincarnated—I am, though you cannot see it, a turtle."

"A turtle!" the boys exclaimed in startled chorus.

"Definitely a turtle. Confronted with the shadow of a threat, I duck back into my shell where I am safe and warm and can concentrate on developing my theory of permanent revolution."

"You are a fine turtle, Papa," Lyova announced.

"And you will be a fine spider, my son." Leaning over my sons' bunk beds, I tucked the blankets under their chins and kissed them good night.

Nata was in the narrow kitchen reheating the meat loaf she and the boys had dined on two hours earlier. I scraped a chair up to the small kitchen table and sat down, happy to take the weight off my feet after the wearisome ride on the overcrowded Third Avenue Elevated. "Your sons didn't want to go to bed until you came home," Nata said, talking to me over her shoulder. "When it grew dark out I had to insist," she told me, spooning meat and potatoes onto one of the plates that was less chipped than the others and putting it down in front of me. "What kept you, Lev?" she asked casually as she filled a tumbler with beer and set it on the table. Then, bending over me, she pulled down the collar of my shirt to peer more closely at my neck. "That's one hell of a reddish blotch you've got," she said.

I touched the spot with the tip of a finger. "It itches a bit," I said.

You're walking on eggs, Litzky warned in my mind's ear. *Keep in mind the best lie is the one that sticks as close as possible to the truth.*

"Were you bitten by an insect?" Nata asked.

"Bukharin took me to see a film with this Chaplin fellow playing the role of a new immigrant. Afterward we met that American Communist, Lou Fraina, I told you about—he was staying, poor fellow, in a dilapidated hotel off Broadway, I suppose because the rooms were cheap. If I was bitten by an insect, it must have happened there." I tried to change the subject. "How was your day, Nata?"

She ignored my question. "Funny, I talked to Bukharin's wife on the telephone this afternoon but she didn't mention the Chaplin film or Lou Fraina."

I concentrated on the meat loaf, washing it down with mouthfuls of beer. "I assume Bukharin doesn't report back to his wife on everything he does."

"I'm not asking you to report back on everything you

do," Nata shot back impatiently. "I am asking you to come home in time to have dinner with your family. I take care of our sons from morning to night—I get them up and washed and dressed while you're still sound asleep, I make them breakfast and walk them to school, I take them to a playground or a zoo after school, in my supposedly free time I shop and cook meals for the four of us. For pity's sake, Lev, the least you could do is read them a story and put them to bed."

I couldn't miss the disagreeable note in her voice. "Life in this weird new country is not a bed of roses for either of us," I reminded her.

"Sorry," she said. "Sorry," she repeated. Then: "I just missed you, Lev."

You really are a son of a bitch, Litzky murmured. *You somehow managed to get her to apologize to you.*

When we went to bed that night I noticed that Nata was wearing the silk nightdress we'd bought in the Paris flea market and not my spare flannel pajamas that were much warmer. We read for twenty or so minutes, she a thin volume of Pushkin poems, me the editorials inside the copy of the *Brooklyn Daily Eagle* that I'd folded into the pocket of my sealskin coat earlier that day. When we both reached to turn out the lamps on the chairs that served as night tables, I said, "Sleep well, my Nata, my victim."

Instead of turning away on her side as she usually did, she pulled the nightdress up over her hips and rolled onto me. "It's been almost three weeks since—" She didn't finish the thought.

"It's late, my dear Nata," I said with a yawn.

"It's so late it's early," she said, repeating what I'd told Lyova when our tramp steamer tied up to the pier at three in the morning. "Don't forget, dearest," she went on, "that it's the early bird that catches the worm." And reaching down to slip a hand under my flannel waistband, she folded her fingers around my worm. "You don't want to waste a serviceable erection, my darling," she added with a slightly anxious giggle.

I heard Litzky, never one to pass up an opportunity to get my goat, yowling into my mind's ear, *Where is it written that you can't make love to one female body while fantasizing about another body? God's nails, get on with it.*

"*Kholera yevo zaberi!*" I said under my breath, almost gagging on the curse directed at my better angel. "*May cholera take you!*"

"May cholera take who?" Nata demanded.

I ad-libbed an explanation: "May cholera take me if I fail to incite revolution in America."

Nata said sullenly, "Ships that pass in the night—I'm talking lovemaking and you're talking revolution!"

"To each, his obsession," I mumbled.

She raised her head off my chest. "Being intimate with one's companion," she informed me icily, "is supposed to come under the heading of gratification, not obsession."

Easing Nata off of me, I scrambled atop her and began to work my way along her body, kissing her nipples and nombril, kissing the birthmark under her right hip and the inside of a thigh before seeking out her genitals with the tip of my newly educated tongue.

Suddenly I felt her hot hand on my head shoving me roughly away. "What the hell do you think you're doing?"

She jerked her legs out from under me and, tugging her nightdress down to her knees, sat back against the wall. "That's disgusting," she said, spitting out the words. "You promised we would be Russian in America. Out of the blue you've turned into a vulgar American in America."

"I have been led to believe the French make love like this," I said, but she had put two and two together.

"You're seeing someone!" she hissed.

I propped myself up beside her, back to the wall. "There's nobody—" I started to say, but she cut me off.

"Don't insult me by denying it. We've been down this road before, Lev: You make no secret about being attracted to beautiful women—that widow of the murdered Socialist in Berlin, that Swiss nurse in Serbia. You've never seen a skirt you haven't looked up, for pity's sake."

"How do you know about the nurse in Serbia?"

"I found one of her letters in the lining of your knapsack."

"Am I on trial?" I demanded.

"When you seek carnal satisfaction outside of our couple, it's me who's on trial!" Nata yanked the blanket up to her neck. "It's the woman who is always on trial when the husband strays. We're trapped in our femininity, Lev. How can you not see it? Women are either seductive or not seductive. You men have alternatives. If you're not good-looking and an athlete in bed, you can fall back on being rich. And if you're not rich, you can fall back on—"

"On?"

"—on making a revolution, on being a revolutionist."

"You're of course oversimplifying—" I started to say but her smoldering monologue, flowing like magma, left no space into which I could slip words.

"I don't begrudge you your itches," she plunged on, though she seemed to be talking to herself as much as to me. "I only ask you not to scratch them under the roof we call our home. I only ask you not to humiliate me by bringing what you do when you fornicate with someone else back into our bed." And with that, she turned away and rolled onto her side.

Was it my imagination or had the ticking of the alarm clock on the chair become deafening? For the longest time we both pretended to be asleep, though neither fooled the other. Then I heard a distant voice, muffled by lips pressed into the pillow, say, "Where has it all gone, dearest heart?"

"Where has what gone, Nata?"

"The scented bird of youth, the fragrant bird of love." She rolled over until her face was almost touching mine. "I smuggled those party congress minutes to Saint Petersburg," she said, "the comrades had to hold the paper over a candle flame for the secret writing to appear, hoping against hope the activist I'd met in Odessa would fall in love with the courier."

"I did fall in love with the courier—"

"That time in Paris when we first lived together—"

"The flat on Rue Lalande—"

"Number Four, Rue Lalande, two floors above the grocery store with the hairless cat that you said looked like a rat. Our bed was so narrow you joked that we'd have to give up eating and stay thin as iron nails if we were going to live under the same roof."

"I'd escaped from Siberia on a luge drawn by reindeer, the little toe on my left foot was still black from frostbite—"

"It was before you let your beard grow."

"We celebrated your twentieth birthday drinking cheap white wine in the alcove that passed for a kitchen."

"You worked for some newspaper—"

"*Nashe Slovo*. I wrote editorials—"

"You were lost in Paris—"

"You took me to the Louvre, to the Luxembourg Gardens, to the Champ de Mars to watch a Zeppelin land, we walked along the Seine embankment in the rain—"

"What happened to us, Lev?"

"Two sons happened to us, Nata. Exile happened to us. Life happened to us."

Her tone hardened. "I was ready to play second fiddle

to the great revolutionist Trotsky—as long as Trotsky was playing first fiddle and not off somewhere fornicating with a chippie."

"I don't love you less for being an accomplished second fiddler, my Nata, my victim. But you have to understand, I'm a man—"

I could see her dark Cossack eyes burning into mine. "That's no excuse," she whispered fiercely.

She turned her back on me. For what seemed like an eternity I concentrated on her shallow breathing, the both of us adrift in an awkward insomnia.

12

I want to set this country on fire to save their lives . . .

IT CREPT UP ON ME on cat's paws—I might not have liked America, scarred by its Indian genocide and its slave trade and its capitalists' obsession with accumulating wealth and transforming human beings into consumers, but I was beginning to like Americans, in a word, to appreciate what the world saw as a flaw of American character: Their innocence!

Comrade Litzky couldn't believe his ears as he breathed into one of mine: *There are Americans living in urban sprawls we call cities who believe chocolate milk comes from brown cows. That doesn't make them innocent, Bronshtein, it makes them stupid.*

Look, I went on, there was something about Americans—oh, I'm not talking about the John E. Hoovers and the so-called Socialist superstars; I'm talking about the working class, what we Marxist-Leninists (yes, yes, I have come to consider myself a Leninist) identified as the proletariat.

Examples, if you please, Litzky insisted. You want examples, I'll give you examples: Starting with my next door neighbor on 1522 Vyse Avenue in the Bronx who turned up to borrow a wedge of margarine from Natalya and volunteered to children sit for us so we could get a rare night out at the Jewish dairy restaurant down the block, starting with the overweight waitress at the Monopole on Second Avenue who dropped the quarter tip Fred left on the table in the cardboard box marked "For our valiant vets," starting with the Jewish dentist Stanley Cohen on the floor above *Novy Mir* who filled a cavity for me but refused to take a dime from a Russian because his father had emigrated from a shtetl in Byelorussia. You get the idea, I'm talking about the ordinary people—the proletarians with threadbare trousers on their legs and worn soles on their shoes and latent rage in their dog-tired eyes—hanging on to overhead straps as the Third Avenue Elevated snakes through the labyrinth called Manhattan to the Bronx. *Excuse my thick-headedness, Bronshtein, but why do you suddenly feel the need to mention this?* I mention it because it has changed my attitude toward revolution in America, I said. *I need to pinch myself! Leon Trotsky is having second thoughts about revolution because he likes some Americans?* Third thoughts and counting, if you're actually keeping track, I said. My confession must have exasperated Litzky because I heard him snicker, *Bog lyubit troitsu—God loves a trinity.* Listen up, I told him, where I once saw myself provoking revolution in this America as a matter of ideology, because I have come to like some Americans, as you so delicately put it, I now see that revolution in America is essential in order to give these good people the thing that's missing from their lives: Hope. I want to free them from the shackles of their racist roots, I want to liberate them from the capitalists and industrialists who oblige them to work twelve-hour shifts in sweatshops. In a word, I want to set this country of theirs on fire to save their lives.

I thought I heard Litzky applauding that very slow, very mocking applause that has haunted me since I first heard it back in the Ukraine when I announced that I planned to quit the safety of my pigsty and follow my father's dictum: When you came to a fork in the road, he had drummed into me from the day he realized I could talk, take the path not paved. Knock off your cynical clapping, I snapped at my conscience, and I turned back to my new and best American friend, Fred, who had a gift for hauling ashes—

Yo, my man Bronshtein is thinking in fluent American now!

Ignoring the interruption in my mind's ear, I concentrated on Fred's gift for hauling ashes that was almost as creative as her inventive slang. She was sitting cross-legged on the other end of the bed, her spine against the peeling paint of the wall, in a kind of postcoital daze. Her peasant blouse, which almost but not quite covered what she called her bush, had slipped off one bare shoulder when she shrugged, which she did on the rare occasions when she couldn't think of what to say. "To answer your question," she finally broke the silence, the lids of her eyes blinking lazily, "I stopped being a Marxist when I understood Karl Heinrich's words were pure unadulterated pie in the sky."

"Pie in the . . ."

"In the sky. Pot of gold at the end of the rainbow. Castles in the air. What the natives in my boondock of Brooklyn call bullshit, for Christ's sake."

"You're deluding yourself," I grumbled, "if you think the true and deep meaning of Communism can be found in the words that Comrade Marx and Comrade Engels used to describe it. The true meaning, the deep meaning, my dear gullible Fred, is in the tone; in the rage that saturates the spaces between their words and inspires the proletariat to class struggle; in the breathless exuberance that deconstructs capitalist fairy tales and stirs comrades to revolution when they realize what the world could be as opposed to what it is."

Making no effort to hide her irritation, Fred said, "I suppose we will just have to agree to disagree. But kindly remember you heard it here: Your notorious dictatorship *of* the proletariat will end up being a dictatorship *over* the proletariat. The social fractures that your glorious revolution were supposed to cure will metastasize—society will be divided into those who believe despite the evidence of their eyes and those who doubt because of the evidence of their eyes."

I would have risen to the occasion and argued with her if I

hadn't been distracted by her grinning that tight-lipped grin of hers. Stretching out one long bare leg, she began to tickle my thigh with her toes. "I'll be damned if this isn't a light bulb moment, Leo: Underneath that intellectual facade of yours, you're just another bleeding-heart Jewish Marxist—"

"I am not a Jewish Marxist. I am a Marxist-Leninist who happens through no fault of his to be Jewish."

"Whichever. But hey, it is a Jewish thing, isn't it, mining the space between the words for the true meaning."

"Jews are not miners," I informed her, "Jews are diamond cutters; we take raw ideas and cut them with painstaking precision into precious concepts that can change history."

Fred shrugged the blouse back onto her naked shoulder. "Hey, I must've worked up an appetite shagging you—and a late lunch is better than no lunch."

"Where are you taking me today?"

"New York is a city of ghettos," she said. "There are neighborhoods crawling with German beer gardens and Irish saloons and Italian trattorias and Jewish delicatessens. But I'm taking you to a juice joint that is one hundred percent Dixieland America. Trust me!"

13

Your Achilles' heel is thinking you don't have one . . .

WITH FRED LEADING THE CARNIVAL, the three of us (the lady herself, yours truly, and my incorrigible conscience) jumped aboard the horsecar headed down Bleecker Street, then caught the Third Avenue Elevated uptown and wound up walking—with Fred's new knee-length skirt turning heads on Fifty-Eighth Street—across town to Columbus Circle and the legendary Reisenweber's Café where, as the quintessential New York saying goes, the elite meet to eat. Feeling flush with her weekly *Brooklyn Eagle* pay envelope in the shirt pocket over her left breast, Fred coughed up the twenty-five cent per head cover charge so we could eat in the swanky second-floor 400 Club and listen to Reisenweber's Original Dixieland Band playing something she identified as ragtime. "'Rag' as in 'ragged,'" Fred—answering my question before I got around to asking it—told me when the musicians chilled out between "rags." "'Ragged' as in 'syncopated.'"

Stirring flurries of sawdust on the floor planks, waiters decked out in white butcher aprons scurried through the rooms miraculously balancing on one palm high over their heads trays filled with food and drinks. Waylaying one of the waiters on his way to the kitchen, Fred got him to take our order and he eventually made his way back with two steins of tap beer and a wooden platter piled with slices of cold pepper steak and a jar of wine mustard. "You happy I took you here, Leo?" Fred demanded, leaning close and shouting into my ear to be heard above the din.

"It's too noisy," I shouted back. "I can barely hear my conscience think."

"For Christ's sake, Leo, that's not noise, that's a new kind of music the Negros in New Orleans call jass—they're playing one of my all-time favorites, 'Livery Stable Blues.'" She gulped down a swig of beer and, leaning toward me again and laughing happily, wiped her lips on my sleeve. "The piano player, the dude in blackface, he's the talk of Broadway, his name is Jimmy Durante but Reisenweber's regulars call him the Schnozzola."

"You want to translate schnozzola into one of the four languages I speak?"

"Schnozzola, as in schnoz, dummy. Schnoz as in nose. Check out his face. Durante is 'the Nose'!"

Two couples began dancing in a space between the tables under the bandstand. "Lookit, Leo—they're doing the 'Turkey Trot.' Want to try?"

Litzky could barely stifle his enthusiasm. *Go for it, Bronshtein. This may be your last best shot at learning to dance.*

I mouthed the words "thanks but no thanks," hoping that Fred would be able to read my lips. Yelling into her ear, I added, "I was too busy taking care of the pigs on my father's farm to learn to dance. And I'm too old to start now."

"You're never too old to be young," she shouted.

I shook my head. "I'm far too old to pretend to be young," I hollered back.

What Fred called jass and I called noise thank goodness came to an end when the Nose and his pals in the band took a cigarette break, though judging from the odor what they were smoking wasn't tobacco. My ears were still ringing after they stopped playing and I had to strain to make out what Fred was ranting about. "Don't tell me you didn't see the story in the newspaper," she cried.

"The one about the czar ordering the Petrograd garrison to crush the women demonstrating for bread?"

"What rabbit's hole do you bury your head in, Leo? The one about Margaret Sanger—they went and arrested her for the crime of running a birth control clinic, for Christ's sake. It figures—the constitution guarantees freedom of speech, so you can say what you want about Woodrow Wilson and his cockamamie idea to organize a League of Nations, but sound off about birth control in puritan America and you wind up in the slammer."

"Another reason why this country of yours needs a revolution," I said. "Is this Sanger person your role model?"

"Ha! Chaucer's Wife of Bath is my role model. You Russians, being hostages of Tolstoy and Dostoevsky, don't know beans about her. I audited my husband's course on this Chaucer character's *Canterbury Tales* last semester, which is how I got myself introduced to the Wife of Bath. Her name's Alison, she had five—count them: Five!—husbands and outlived them all, including the last one who was twenty years younger than her. The real revolution, my dear naive Leo, will come when an army of women rise up against state and church-organized misogyny. Now that you've added 'schnozzola' to your imperfect English, you'll need to wrestle with 'misogyny.' Saint Paul, the original misogynist, decreed that women should not be allowed to speak in church, so the story goes, which is how come the Roman Catholic bishops in their infinite wisdom decided females couldn't become priests."

Pin her down, Litzky suggested. *Ask what the ladies expect from this revolution against church and state.*

"Educate me, Fred: What exactly do women expect from this revolution against church and state?"

"Women expect to get what Alison took for granted—sovereignty over our bodies, sovereignty over our lovers and husbands who assume an erection gives them a free pass to our vaginas."

"Not equality?"

"Sovereignty, Leo, implies equality and then some."

For want of anything to say, I uttered "Right."

The telltale grin materialized on Fred's face. "Right as rain," she agreed.

She doesn't come from planet earth, this half Mexican, half Jewish journalist friend of yours. What is right about rain?

I couldn't resist putting Litzky's question to Fred. "And what, pray tell, is right about rain?"

"Unlike the air we breathe, unlike the food we eat or the lives we lead, unlike the revolutions we make or break in my dad's Mexico or your czar's Russia, rain has the saving grace of being pure."

"In my father's pigsty, rain was a calamity—our pigs wallowed in the mud, we had to hose them down before we slaughtered them if we hoped to market the meat."

She regarded me, her eyes squinting thoughtfully. "I'm trying to imagine you as a kid in your father's muddy pigsty, hosing down pigs, Leo. What were you really like, a Jewish boy in an Orthodox country raising non-kosher meat?"

Here's the thing: To my stupefaction, Fred's question suddenly triggered in me a sense of aching homesickness. "Kosher had nothing to do with it," I exclaimed. "My father grew corn, which had the disadvantage of needing a lot of water, and beetroot, which had the advantage of being a seven-week crop. One summer when I was eight he tried to grow barley in the south field but the crop was wiped out by stem rust and he never planted barley again. He raised cows until he discovered there was a market for pork, at which point he switched to pigs."

"You don't answer my question."

"What was I like? As far back as I can remember I fantasized about running away from home, from school, from the Russian kids who taunted the rare Jew in Yanofska as a Christ-killer, from my chores hosing down pigs in the muddy pigsty."

"Did you? Run away from home?"

"When I was old enough to be drafted into the Russian army, I put my father's pigsty behind me and became a professional revolutionist, always on the run to stay one step ahead of the czar's Okhrana. When I was a kid I escaped into my imagination."

"What did you imagine?"

"I imagined success with the girls, though I defined success as sweet-talking a girl down to the peat moss riverbank of the Dnipro and pretending to be interested in the stars while I casually slipped my hand onto her hip. When I reached puberty I imagined what that success really looked like—what it looked like was the female body, in its glorious nakedness, at my fingertips."

"And now that you're too old to be young?"

I turned to watch the Nose and his band flicking cigarette ends into a spittoon as they meandered back onto the small stage. "Nowadays, with age," I said, "I imagine stirring a Socialist revolution in some country." I looked her in the eye. "Any country, actually, starting with America."

Fred snickered. "Your dream of revolution, Leo, has something in common with your father's barley: It will never take root in American soil."

I heard Litzky say *I'm beginning to suspect she may be right.* And hearing this from both Fred and my conscience-in-residence, I suddenly realized that I, too, doubted revolution in America was in the cards—the doubt had infected a lobe of my brain and left me more pessimistic than I was comfortable admitting, even to myself, about what I could accomplish during my American exile.

Fred must have spotted the shadow of a doubt in my eyes. "Hey, cheer up, Leo, forget revolution for a minute and concentrate on the soon-to-be naked female body at your sweaty fingertips."

"One doesn't exclude the other," I said with less conviction than I would normally have been able to muster.

"One may exclude the other," she shot back—she had to shout to finish her thought as the rag they called music started up—"if you become a victim of this revolution you dream of stirring up."

At the next cigarette break, we were both waving to get the attention of a waiter and order refills when a clotheshorse in a three-piece off-white suit and white buckskins, with shocks of grey hair falling over his enormous ears, stopped by our table with a gorgeous Ziegfeld blonde in tow. “Long time no see, Fred,” he gushed. “Where y’all been hidin’ that finger-lickin’ butt of yours?”

“In my boondock Brooklyn, is where. Yo, Furman, I heard you were doing time in the hoosegow.”

“Ayuh, did my time, darlin’, not fixin’ on doing more time till the cows come home.”

“Cows come home when the sun sets, honeybunch?” the Ziegfeld girl, visibly inebriated, cooed.

“Aren’t you going to introduce your tomato?” Fred asked.

Furman chortled. “Fact is I do not recollect her name.”

“Dagnabbit, Furman, there you go again,” the blonde squealed, “peein’ down my back and tellin’ me it’s rainin’.” She turned to Fred. “Name’s Marybeth, sugar-pie, and daddy here damn well knows it.”

“Don’t pay her no mind,” Furman said. “She’s cuter than cat’s whiskers when she’s sober.” He took a long hard look at me. “Who be your friend?” he asked Fred.

She coughed up a laugh. “Unlike you I happen to remember names,” she told him. “His is Leo. Leo Trotsky. He’s a famous Russian.”

“What he be famous for?”

“He’s famous for presiding over the first Russian soviet after the 1905 revolution. More recently he’s famous for wanting to preside over the first American soviet here in the U.S. of A.”

“Never met me a Russian before,” Furman allowed.

I joined the conversation, if you could call it a conversation.

"Makes us even," I said. "I never met a Southern gentleman before."

"Don't like him," Furman decided, looking at me but talking to Fred.

"Why?"

"Trotsky strikes me as a Jew name. Back home in Alabama we got us a timeworn saw: If it ain't broke, don't fix it. America ain't broke. Don't hold with the Jewish trying to fix what ain't broke."

Fred shut her eyes in exasperation. "It has surely slipped your feeble mind that I happen to be half Jewish."

Furman raised an eyebrow. "Well then, darlin', there it is, set out without Christmas wrappin' for all who come equipped with eyes to see—this 'half Jewish, half not' of yours be a fatal flaw, what y'all call an Achilles' heel."

Marybeth looked confused. "Who the heck is Achilles, daddy, and why is he a heel?"

I piped up. "Achilles was a Greek dude," I said, but I didn't get the feeling my explanation solved the mystery for her.

Furman and his Ziegfeld chum thank God moved on, and Fred and I, at a loss for words, concentrated on our steins of beer. "Hey, Leo," she said, breaking the suddenly icy silence, "in your scheme of things, does everyone have an Achilles' heel?"

Eggshell alert, Bronshtein, Litzky breathed in my ear. *Walk on them at your own risk.*

I nodded. "In my experience, yes, almost everyone has an Achilles' heel."

"Do I have an Achilles' heel?"

I nodded again—carefully.

"Okay, then. Identify my Achilles' heel."

"Sex, obviously. You're obsessed with it. You talk about it all the time. You practice it when you can find someone to practice on. You dread the day when you'll no longer be sexually attractive, which you think of as a kind of death before dying."

Fred digested what I'd said. "What about you?" she demanded. "Identify your Achilles' heel."

"I don't have one."

"Ha! That there's your Achilles' heel, Leo—thinking you don't have one!"

I thought I heard Litzky's inimitable chortle in my mind's ear.

"What?" I demanded.

"What *what*?" Fred said.

"I wasn't talking to you."

"Oh."

14

Only Socialist revolution can resurrect the dead . . .

COOPER UNION'S FAN-SHAPED GREAT HALL was awash with what my crank of a conscience, as incurable a snob as ever set foot in an emporium of higher learning, thought of as the great unwashed: Union rank and file in bib-and-brace Levi Strauss overalls, undergraduates in coarse Indian dungri, faculty in various shades of grey flannel, street sweepers in soiled yellow boiler suits, salesgirls from Mr. Macy's Herald Square department store in identical ankle-length culotte skirts. There was even a smattering of what I took to be Bowery alcoholics wearing a hotchpotch of threadbare corduroy and willing to sit through even the devil's speech if it sheltered them, for an hour or two, from the gusting March thunderstorm drenching Lower Manhattan. "It gives me a great deal of personal satisfaction," Algernon Lee, the director of the Rand School for Social Research, was bellowing into the microphone as I fidgeted in discomfort on one of the folding metal chairs behind the lectern, "to introduce a distinguished Russian freedom fighter here in an auditorium where Abraham Lincoln and Mark Twain and Susan B. Anthony once captivated audiences. Our guest's reputation precedes him and I can assure you you won't regret being out of pocket the fifteen-cent entrance fee." Lee waved a hand, summoning me to the microphone. "Friends, please welcome Leon Trotsky!"

People leaped to their feet to give me a standing ovation, which encouraged me to believe I wasn't wasting my time and breath turning up at Cooper Union. I breasted the applause as if it were a wave, and when it persisted I motioned for everyone to take their seats. As the clapping and foot-stamping petered out, I spotted Fred beaming at me from the second row—she had an aisle seat, which afforded me a glimpse of her delicious knees. Tapping the microphone to be sure it was still working, I saluted the audience. "Ladies and gentlemen," I said—and immediately noticed the sullen expressions on the faces peering up at me. Litzky, his bated breath scorching my inner ear, chided me, *Yipes, Bronshtein, since when do you greet an auditorium crawling with Socialists with ladies and gentlemen!* I took his point and started again. "Comrades!" I cried, "I greet you in the name of the world proletariat and the revolution gathering over the heads of their capitalist exploiters like a storm cloud about to burst." With that the clapping and the foot-stamping began anew. When silence had finally settled on the auditorium, I threw myself into the speech that I had rehearsed with Nata the night before. "As many of you may know, this building at Cooper Union was the first in the world to be constructed with an elevator shaft—that happened in 1859, long before an elevator existed. Mr. Cooper, himself an inventor who I'm told made his first fortune running a glue factory, was betting that the elevator would be invented. Which is another way of saying he imagined the future before the present caught up with it. I, too, imagine the future. Like Mr. Cooper and his elevator shaft fifty-eight years ago, I imagine the political thunderstorm looming just over the horizon." *Slow down, Bronshtein, take a deep breath and milk the applause*, Litzky spluttered into my inner ear. I paused until the clapping and foot-stamping died down again. "Europe," I continued, "has become a kingdom of stagnation—it is transforming itself into a giant cemetery for the workers who are on each end of the blood-whetted bayonet."

Blood-whetted! Rousing the rabble with poetry, are we, Bronshtein? Litzky sneered.

"Comrades, an ocean of blood has been shed, three million Russian soldiers have been transformed into corpses, the workers, the peasants have lost their illusions and their innocence. Socialist revolution is festering in the trenches. Only Socialist revolution can resurrect the dead," I roared into the microphone to be heard over the bedlam rising from the Great Hall. Half the people in the audience were on their feet cheering. I gestured for quiet. "Mark my words, comrades: Socialist revolution is coming to Russia!"

A Negro two rows behind Fred climbed onto his seat. "We're not Russia here," he shouted. "What about America, Trotsky?"

"America, too, is impatient to chuck the capitalist model into the dustbin of history," I exclaimed. "Rev-oh-lu-tion is in the air you breathe, my friend. Your President Wilson's formula—'peace without victory'—won't solve anything. It would leave the kaiser's Germany in possession of territories it occupied in Russia and Belgium and France and sow the seeds of yet another great war."

Litzky couldn't resist nagging me. *Correct me if I'm wrong, Bronshtein, but you've never actually had a conversation with a Negro before, have you?*

There weren't any on my father's farm in the Ukraine to talk to, I reminded my conscience. Ditto the Realschule gymnasium in Odessa. Or in Siberian exile for that matter.

An eerie calm had settled over the auditorium. The Negro, still standing on his seat, called out, "Comrade Trotsky here seems to have convinced himself that America is ripe for revolution. Wishful thinking won't make it so!"

"Wishful thinking," I said quietly—my hoarse voice reverberating through the Great Hall from loudspeakers—"brought elevators into Mr. Cooper's elevator shaft."

Applause flooded the auditorium. Algernon Lee came over and planted moist kisses on both my cheeks. "From your lips to God's ears," he gushed.

They had organized a post-speech reception in the Cooper Union's canteen for the happy few. Flashing her *Brooklyn Daily Eagle* press pass, Fred sweet-talked her way past the two matrons guarding the sanctum from the hoi polloi and, hoisting herself onto a table—oh, those knees again!—watched me fending off the reporters. Dipping a tin mug into the giant glass bowl filled with something the Americans called punch, I turned back to the gaggle shouting questions.

"Having escaped from one of the czar's Siberian prisons, do you plan to settle permanently in America, Mr. Trotsky?"

"I see myself returning to Mother Russia when Czar Nicholas is unemployed and his Siberian prisons have been razed to the ice-glazed steppe."

Blood-whetted! Ice-glazed! What have you been smoking, Bronshtein?

"Apart from fomenting revolution, what is it you really want out of life, Mr. Trotsky?" a gentleman with a twitching walrus mustache called out.

"I want to be the first to climb the highest mountain in Russia, Mount El'brus in the Caucuses."

"Mr. Trotsky, Mr. Trotsky, over here: Why is it so important to be the first?"

Mind your tongue, Bronshtein, lest you provide that Freud fellow in Vienna with the key to your libido.

Flouting Litzky's warning, I decided to answer the question. "I want to be the first"—I couldn't miss Fred egging me on with one of her tight-lipped grins—"because nobody will remember the name of the second."

"So it's fame you're being after, then?" a woman with what I took to be an Irish accent hollered.

"It's revolution I'm after," I replied heatedly. "If the revolution happens to make me famous, I will wear the fame with dignity and make good use of it to inspire sister revolutions."

"If the bleedin' past coughs up clues to the present day, you are more likely to be infamous than famous," the woman, smirking, declared.

"Russian peasants say the past is unpredictable," I told the woman. She laughed along with everyone else crowding around the table—including Litzky. I could hear the old nag of a better angel chortling in my ear. *Ha! She's saying exactly what I said the day you set foot in the New World. I am able to read the handwriting on the wall, Bronshtein: You may start off merely famous, but if you refuse to be guided by your conscience you are destined to wind up infamous.*

I would havc put Litzky in his place if the three men in identical coal black suits pushing through the crowd hadn't caught my eye. "Leon Trotsky," one of them intoned, "we have a warrant for your arrest."

"What for? For what?"

"For sedition. For inciting law-abiding Americans to riot against the authority of the state."

Algernon Lee attempted to intervene. "On whose authority are you arresting him?"

The first agent waved a scrap of paper in Algernon's face. "On the authority of the Unites States government."

Fred slid off her perch on the table and grabbed hold of my arm. One of the agents made a show of prying her fingers off me, one at a time. "Interfering with an agent of the Bureau of Investigation in the lawful performance of his duty is a misprision of a felony, miss."

"Screw you," Fred said with a scowl. The people around the table, Socialists to a fault, cheered her on. The agent shoved her roughly back, then produced handcuffs and slipped them onto my wrists so adroitly I didn't have time to pull my hands away. Grasping the chain between the two cuffs as if it were a dog leash, pulling me along behind him while the two other agents parted the Red Sea of Socialists, he headed for the door. "I'll have you out on bail in an hour," Algernon Lee shouted at our retreating backs.

"Pigs will fly, hell will freeze over before you get out on bail," the agent holding my leash muttered.

The rear door of the black limousine with tinted windows parked at the curb flew open as we approached. One of the agents pushed my head down and shoved me onto the back seat. Two agents slid in on either side of me. As the motor coughed into life and the car edged into the traffic on Third Avenue, the figure sitting next to the driver turned toward me. "I had a feeling our paths would cross again," he said.

"Well, if it isn't Mr. Hoover from the Bureau of Investigation," I said.

He didn't smile. "One and the same," he said.

"Put your head between your knees," the agent sitting on my right ordered.

"There's no way I'm putting my head—"

The other agent sucker punched me in the solar plexus. I produced a stifled scream of agony and, doubling over, my head between my knees, vomited on my shoes.

"Holy shit," the agent who had punched me said.

"You ought not to have hit him so hard," Hoover told him with a laugh.

"Live and learn, Chief," the agent said.

Given the revolting stench in the car, Mr. Hoover and his agents were as relieved as I was to arrive at their destination somewhere in Lower Manhattan. I could sense the limousine descending a ramp into an underground garage. None too soon, the agents hauled me out of the car and into an open freight elevator, which ascended to the seventh floor. I was forced to remove my belt and my shoelaces, and empty my pockets onto a tabletop, then pushed into a windowless cell with a metal army cot along one wall fitted with wooden planks where the mattress should have been, and a toilet without a lid. "I need water to clean my trousers and my shoes," I called to one of the agents.

"Water's in the toilet bowl," he said with a smirk.

"You expect me to use water from a toilet bowl?" I said. "Even the czar's prisons had running water for their guests."

"Your call," the agent said. "Use it, don't use it, no skin off my nose either way."

He slammed the door shut behind him and I could hear a bolt being thrown. And high above my head—beyond the reach of my hands—a single light bulb brightened intensely. Being a veteran of the czar's prisons, I understood what was going on: Police techniques are universal and the bright light, the cot without a mattress, were intended to deprive me of sleep. Some hours later—I'd lost track of time; lost track of whether it was day or night—a tin bowl filled with slop was shoved through a small opening in the door. Retrieving the tin bowl, I emptied the slop into the toilet and flushed it, and used the bowl to scoop up water and wipe the traces of vomit off my trousers and shoes. Suddenly parched, I filled the bowl with water from the toilet and drank it off—all the while staring defiantly at the peephole set high on the door of my cell.

"I can see from your comportment, Trotsky, that you have experienced incarceration before," Hoover greeted me at what turned out to be the first of several interrogations. I'd been led through a narrow corridor that reeked of floor polish and stale air to another windowless room and shoved onto a kitchen chair. Mr. Hoover presided from behind a ridiculously small desk fitted with an old-fashioned inkwell. A gentleman impeccably dressed in a tweed suit, with a short military haircut and long sideburns that curled around his flushed cheeks, looked on from a corner of the room.

"One never becomes accustomed to incarceration," I said. "The czar's Okhrana agents were obviously more skillful than you. When they sat a prisoner on a chair they were careful to shorten its front legs so he was uncomfortable during the interrogation."

"Thank you for the pointer, Trotsky. I shall bring it to the attention of my superiors."

"Last time we met you were letting me into the country so I could radicalize the Socialists to discredit them in the eyes of the great unwashed. That's what I was doing. What's changed?"

"He evidently hasn't seen the latest telegrams from Europe," the gentleman with sideburns said.

"Yesterday, the eighth of March in the year of our Lord 1917," Mr. Hoover said, "food riots broke out in the Russian capital of Petrograd. Army units that were dispatched by the czar to quell the riots mutinied and joined the demonstrators. Your czar is rushing back from the front but the railroad workers have stalled his train and are demanding he abdicate. Our British friends fear he will. Which makes you, according to the Brits, the most dangerous man in New York: If the czar does abdicate, which appears more likely by the hour, your Lenin and his lickspittle bootlicker Trotsky will try to seize power and take Russia out of the war, which would be a disaster for both the British and the French. So they prevailed on us to remove you from circulation until things settle down and we can see which way the wind is blowing in Russia."

Suppressing the upwelling of sheer joy I felt at hearing the news from Petrograd, I turned to look across the room at the gentleman with the sideburns. "I take it you are one of his British friends."

"You will forgive me if I don't introduce myself," the gentleman remarked.

I turned back to Mr. Hoover. "I was led to believe that in these United States, you can't simply take someone out of circulation."

"Tell it to a judge—if you see a judge," Mr. Hoover snapped. A smirk distorted his face. "You are in a great deal of hot water, Trotsky. There are laws in these United States against inciting people to riot."

"I was trying to incite them to revolution, not riot."

"Riot, revolution, two sides of the same coin. You were attempting to destabilize the United States of America, one nation, indivisible, with liberty and justice for all." Mr. Hoover addressed the gentleman with sideburns. "One day we hope to get Congress to add 'under God' to our lovely pledge of allegiance."

"Under which God?" I demanded.

Mr. Hoover looked startled. "Come again?"

"One nation under which God, Mr. Hoover?"

"Under what the Hebrews in the Old Testament called Yahweh: *the* God, the one God." Mr. Hoover's eyelids drifted closed as he recited: "*Sh'ma Yisrael, Adonaï Eloheinu Adonaï Eḥad.*"

Hell's bells—the son of a bitch is Jewish! Litzky gasped in my ear.

"Are you by any chance Jewish?" I inquired.

Mr. Hoover's eyes flicked open. "Not that it is any concern of yours but I happen to be, like our President Wilson, a practicing Presbyterian. Like Protestants in general, we Presbyterians, spiritually speaking, acknowledge our Jewish roots."

I was beginning to enjoy the conversation with the Neanderthal who ran the Bureau of Investigation. "I happen to be a practicing atheist," I explained, leaning forward in my chair, "but I have long concluded that your one God is the heart of the problem. When people worshipped—prayed to—many gods, each tribe to its own God, the world was more or less able to survive what Karl Marx correctly called the opiate of the people: Religion. But your one-God syndrome will be the unmaking of civilization, because if you seriously believe there is only one God, you are more or less compelled to make everyone worship your God. And when they refuse, you are more or less obliged to declare them to be heretics and kill them. How many humans have had their lives cut short by religious fanatics trying to convert them to their *one* God? Masses. Millions."

Mr. Hoover sank back into his seat. "You are, I admit, a curious bird, Trotsky. I never expected to discuss religion with a Marxist—"

The gentleman with the sideburns in the corner cleared

his throat. "Indeed, I was hoping to witness something more pertinent than a philosophic discussion of religion between a Marxist Jew and a capitalist Presbyterian," he said.

They called you a Marxist, Litzky tut-tutted in my ear. *It behooves you to set the record straight, Bronshtein.*

I spoke up. "I identify as a Marxist-Leninist, with the emphasis on Leninist."

"Ah, that makes a world of difference," Sideburns said. "Marx, my dear Hoover, was merely a wretched theorist who twisted history into a Gordian knot in an effort to make some sort of economic sense. Trotsky's Lenin expects to make his curtain call as a practicer of carnage committed in the name of this antediluvian Marxist knot."

Did you catch the English accent? Litzky whispered.

It dawned on me that Mr. Hoover was not the senior person in this room. Sideburns was. "You speak with an English accent," I noted.

"I am English to the marrow of my bones, Mr. Trotsky. And damn proud of it."

"You wouldn't be Sir William Wiseman, Britain's top intelligence constable in New York, would you? Socialists who speak of you say that you have your shoelaces ironed every morning and a soldier's ramrod up your English arse."

The corners of Sideburns's pursed lips unfolded into a razor-thin smile. "If I might suggest," he said—in a voice so soft I suddenly realized he was pulling rank on Mr. Hoover—"your Mr. Trotsky is too wide awake, John. If in fact he has been communicating with this chap Lenin, he is not going to tell us about it tonight no matter how long he sits in this pew. We may be able to worm a bit more out of him if he were to be deprived of sleep for a day or two or three. Fatigue, my dear John, in my experience loosens bowels and tongues."

Which is how I came to spend interminable hours (also uncountable, inasmuch as my trusty Swiss pocket watch had been confiscated) twisting and turning on the wooden planks of my cot desperately trying to shield my eyes from the brilliant overhead light with a forearm, trying also to plug my topside ear with a fingertip to keep from hearing the nasal bawl of their President Wilson being piped into my cell reading, over and over, something called the Declaration of Independence, whatever that was. At the beginning of the ordeal I fought off grogginess by engaging in bitchy conversations with my conscience, but Litzky became less and less responsive as the hours of cruel sleeplessness wore on; for once his heart—or should I say *our* hearts!—weren't in it. Hoping to make time pass more quickly, I summoned images of Fred the very first time I saw her without clothes on, but her face and body quickly morphed into images of Natalya with, curiously, clothes on. Looking back I can see now that my desperate attempts to decipher the messages my brain in its infinite fatigue was sending, more than the dull drone of President Wilson's voice or the excruciating hardness of the planks under my hip, were what kept me from drifting off into the relative safety of sleep, even for the blink of an eyelid.

"So, Trotsky," the Englishman I took for William Wiseman was saying, "whilst in France you edited the Paris newspaper *Nashe Slovo*, which ran articles calling on the workers to root for defeat of their own countries, inasmuch as defeat would create the conditions for revolution. You mined pretty much the same theme in your articles here, not to mention your speeches to various Socialist audiences. I take it you have been in touch with your Vladimir Lenin whilst you were a refugee in these United States."

It was my second—or perhaps third, or for all I know tenth—interrogation; I had lost track somewhere along the way—though I am quite certain it was the Englishman sitting behind the ridiculously small desk who posed the questions while the young John E. Hoover, forever sucking on one of his foul-smelling cigarillos, lurked in a corner of the stuffy room.

"If I could sleep for one minute, not more," I pleaded in a voice so thick with fatigue I barely recognized it was me speaking.

Sideburns raised his eyes to study the ceiling. "Sleep that knits up the raveled sleeve of care, the death of each day's life," he proclaimed as if he were reciting some famous poem.

I shook my head to dispel the cobwebs. "Corresponding with Lenin is not a criminal offense," I insisted.

"I am not suggesting it was a criminal offense," Sideburns

said soothingly. "We would simply like to understand his intentions if and when he assumes power in Russia."

"You are interested in his program?"

"Indeed."

"I can tell you that his first order of business—"

In your stupor, be wary not to spill state secrets, Litzky—as drowsy as I was, judging from his tone—whined into my inner ear.

"Be a good fellow, do go on, Trotsky. Lenin's first order of business interests us enormously. Don't you agree, John?"

From his perch in the corner of the room, Mr. Hoover played along with the Englishman running the show. "Your Vladimir Lenin would surely want the world to appreciate his first order of business," he suggested.

"If you really think the world would profit from this information—"

"I most certainly do think that," Sideburns said. "And you will feel unburdened when you tell us."

"His first order of business, when we Bolsheviks seize power and Comrade Lenin becomes czar of all the Russians, will be to reform the Russian alphabet and simplify spelling."

"The bastard is pulling our legs," Mr. Hoover snarled from the wall.

"Reforming the alphabet, simplifying spelling," I sleepwalked on, numb from fatigue but scouring my brain to retrieve Lenin's exact words, "more than arcane economic restructuring that puts the means of production into the hands of the relatively few urban proletarians, will attract hordes of illiterate peasants to the Bolshevik cause."

"That's it?" Sideburns said pleasantly. "Not summary executions, not banishing his opponents to some Siberian steppe, not ending hostilities and concluding a separate peace with the kaiser's Germany?"

"Not," I agreed tiredly.

"Oh, dear, I confess that's not quite what I expected from your Vladimir Lenin," Sideburns admitted.

When I think back on this scene now, I remember being struck by Sideburns's genuine disappointment; hoping for red meat he had gotten his paws on rotting fish. I remember also the door of the room flying open and a young woman rushing in to thrust a sheet of paper into his hand. In my mind's eye I see him carefully fitting a pair of steel-rimmed spectacles onto his long English nose and bending over the paper, I hear him pronouncing words that I'd never before heard and didn't quite get the gist of: "Bloody hell!" is what he said.

I remember thinking, in my stupor, that Sideburns must have at one point in his life visited hell. How else could he have known it was bloody?

I remember Mr. Hoover peering over his shoulder. "It's a writ of habeas corpus," he said. "It appears to have been submitted by Algernon Lee's lawyer and signed by one of the judges on the Marxist-infested New York appellate court. I'm afraid, William, we have no choice in the matter—we've got to turn the bastard loose."

Litzky's exhausted voice filled my brain. *I'm out of here!* he cried, celebrating his own liberation more than mine.

I understood what a writ of habeas corpus signified and, sitting awkwardly on the kitchen chair with its front legs newly shortened, promptly shut my eyes and, my numb arms flailing, plummeted headfirst into an ocean of sleep.

15

Lenin said there are weeks when decades happen . . .

"TELL ME THE TRUTH, FOR once," Natalya breathed in a stifled undertone so the boys, sleeping in the next room, wouldn't hear us quarrelling. "Nikolai Bukharin phoned to say you'd been detained—that was the word he used. Detained by whom, I asked. Your pal didn't know. Detained where, I asked. He didn't know that either. God knows I want to believe Nikolai. God knows I want to believe you—but I wasn't born yesterday, Lev. If there's a woman—"

"It's not what you think, Nata," I groaned, still woozy from my incarceration. "How long have I been gone?"

"The question is not how long, though it was three full days and, more to the point, three full nights," Natalya said. "The question is: Where were you?"

I described, again, the underground garage, the freight elevator, the cell with its brilliant overhead lightbulb, as well as the toilet without a lid and the wooden planks on an army cot instead of a mattress, thinking the sheer weight of the details would convince her I was telling the God's honest truth. But she had persuaded herself, long before I staggered through the doorway of our Bronx apartment—unshaven, disheveled, tufts of matted hair on my aching head, my fly half-open, the filthy tails of my once-white shirt trailing behind me like a wake—that I'd spent the three days and three nights with someone she identified as "that woman." I kept feeding her details as they surfaced in my brain—the sucker punch, the vomit I'd washed off my shoes and trousers with water from the toilet bowl, the peephole high in the door of the cell, President Wilson's nasal bawl being piped into the room—in the hope of changing her mind. And then I stumbled on the single detail that made a dent in her suspicions: I described how I kept sliding off the kitchen chair with its front legs newly shortened—shortened because I had alerted this John E. Hoover fellow to the Okhrana's interrogation techniques.

Nata's mouth opened and she gasped, "You couldn't have invented that!" And she flung her arms around my neck still stiff from being curled up on boards instead of a mattress. "I don't know what got hold of me, Lev. I was worried sick." She trembled with silent laughter.

"When I was desperate to escape into sleep, Nata, my love, my victim, I summoned an image of you."

"Why do you think they arrested you? For pity's sake, what could you possibly have told them that they couldn't find in the newspaper?"

The two of us settled onto kitchen chairs to read and reread the glorious headlines on the *New York Times* front page that sounded to both our ears like a triumphant medieval call to arms. She had torn out the page and spread it on the kitchen table, weighing it down in the corners with salt and pepper cellars and kitchen tumblers. I ran my fingers across the headlines as if they were written in braille as I read, again, the words that would change our lives and our children's. REVOLUTION IN RUSSIA; CZAR ABDICATES; EMPRESS IN HIDING; DUMA DEPUTIES FORM PROVISIONAL GOVERNMENT AND BEGIN ISSUING DECREES.

"I remember Lenin saying there are decades when nothing happens and weeks when decades happen," I said. "We are living in such a week now." I felt the blistering breath of Litzky scorching my mind's ear. "We need to go home," I told Nata.

Her silent laughter that had something in common with weeping resurfaced. "I was getting used to the crazy idea that we might grow old in a foreign country called the Bronx . . ." With a shudder, Nata collected herself. "But how on earth shall we be able to go back, my darling? We scrimp every penny as it is to pay the rent and put food on the table for ourselves and the boys. Where will we find money to buy passage for four on a ship sailing to Russia and the revolution?"

16

Wouldn't be good manners to be late to the revolution . . .

WHEN I FINALLY MADE IT to *Novy Mir*'s basement workplace the next morning—a good hour and a quarter late because I had slept through Nata's alarm clock ringing on the chair next to the bed and her exasperated entreaties to stir—my great friend Nikolai Bukharin was clearing out his desk and stuffing his belongings into an army surplus rucksack.

"You're leaving?" I asked—though I knew the answer.

"I'm going home, comrade," he said excitedly.

"How?"

He lowered his voice so as not to be overheard by the others, milling raucously around the brand-new coffee percolator across the room. "I figure I'll cross America by train, then book passage on a tramp steamer to Japan. I'm sure to find a way back to Siberia from Japan. And then the Trans-Siberian across Russia to Petrograd and the revolution."

At the coffee percolator, the *Novy Mir* regulars were chatting breathlessly. Snatches of conversation reached our ears.

"I heard that millions of peasants deserted to return to the land for the harvest . . ."

"They say the women in the streets demanding bread were shouting Bolshevik slogans . . ."

"Their sons and husbands in the Petrograd garrison, God bless them, refused to obey orders to crush the protests . . ."

Nikolai looked at me, clearly distressed. "I've been hoarding pennies against this day. But I only have one fare to worry about—you, four."

"Don't feel guilty," I told him. "All of us need to figure out how to join the revolution as soon as we can."

Nikolai laughed that raucous laugh of his. "Wouldn't be good manners to be late to the revolution, would it?" He turned serious. "If I could help you—"

"You would. I know."

Two old comrades on the precipice of an apocalypse, we threw our arms around one another. "We will meet in Petrograd," I promised.

"Yes, yes, for sure, in Petrograd we will meet to organize revolution and the world's first worker's state."

The bell above the basement's street door jingled and a rail-thin Negro wearing an earring in one lobe and the distinctive black suit and cap of a chauffeur hesitated on the threshold. *Novy Mir*'s editor in chief, my old Petersburg pal Gregory Weinstein, shouted, "Come on the hell in," and in he came.

"I'm looking for a Mr. Trotsky," he said.

Nikolai, chuckling, grabbed hold of my wrist and raised it. The chauffeur retrieved a sealed envelope from his breast pocket and handed it to me. My name was on the envelope, written in a beautiful script that resembled calligraphy. *For the right honorable revolutionist Leon Trotsky, for his eyes only*, it said. I tore open the envelope and, with Nikolai peering over my shoulder despite the "for his eyes only" injunction, read the note. "With the abdication of the czar, I expect you will be chafing at the bit to return to Russia," it said. "I am able to help you. I invite you to share a pastrami sandwich with me in Washington Square Park, Mr. Trotsky. I shall be on a bench near the Waverly Place entrance, a copy of your *Novy Mir* beside me. Twelve noon. Kindly don't keep me waiting."

The note was signed but unlike the text, which probably had been written by a secretary, the signature was illegible. "Who employs you?" I asked the Negro, hoping to decipher the name of the author of this letter.

"Why, my employer employs me," he replied with a big grin.

"And who be your employer?" Bukharin demanded.

"Last time I looked it be Mr. Zylberstein," he said.

"Asher Zylberstein, the Jewish aluminum magnate," Nikolai said. "He's so well-heeled he is said to rent a suite at the Waldorf-Astoria by the year." Nikolai snickered. "You're not a virgin when it comes to dealing with filthy rich capitalists. What do you have to lose?"

I spotted the copy of *Novy Mir* on the park bench (it turned out to be folded around a thick pastrami sandwich on rye) next to Asher Zylberstein, unshaven and dressed in shabby corduroy trousers and a duffel coat that had weathered one storm too many. He looked to be pushing seventy from the wrong side, as they say. Strands of silky grey hair escaped the seaman's watch cap on his skull. "You will be the gentleman who sent me an invitation to share his lunch," I guessed, planting myself in front of him.

"And you, my dear, will be the world-famous Leon Trotsky," he said with a wry chuckle.

"There are some who describe me as world-infamous," I said, settling onto the bench next to him.

"I suspect what separates world-famous from world-infamous is how you deal with a hereditary monarch ruling with an iron fist a vast country like Russia. Are you up for half a delectable pastrami sandwich, Mr. Trotsky? It comes from the famous—given how much they charge for their sandwiches, I should probably say infamous—Katz's kosher delicatessen on Houston and Ludlow. As a practicing revolutionist who happens to be a nonpracticing Jew, you have nothing against eating kosher, I trust?"

"I also eat kosher," I told him.

Asher Zylberstein laughed under his breath. "I like you," he said. "A nonobservant Jew who also eats kosher is someone with two feet planted in the real world." He pried open a pearl-handled pocket knife, carefully cut the sandwich in two, and offered me half. Having raced out of our Bronx apartment without breakfast, I was actually famished and bit into it with relish. Asher Zylberstein munched on his half, cleaning his teeth—two of them glistening gold—with his tongue between bites. I couldn't help but notice he appeared to have names inked on the palm of one hand. He noticed me noticing. "I never forget a face, Mr. Trotsky, but as I am no longer a spring chicken I find it difficult to come up with names to match the face. The names of my staff, my collaborators, even the names of my seven grandchildren that were once lodged in my memory seem to have migrated to the tip of my tongue, where they appear to be stuck."

"You don't dress like someone who has a chauffeur," I said, talking with my mouth full.

"I have a limousine to go with the chauffeur, dear boy. It's a Hudson Super Six which accelerates—hold on to the seat of your pants, Mr. Trotsky—from zero to sixty in under a minute. Oh dear, if I knew how to drive one of these Hudson thingamajigs you can bet your bottom dollar I'd be chauffeuring my chauffeur, not vice versa."

"It's never too late to learn."

"They say you can't teach an old dog new tricks," he observed wistfully.

A young woman with the hem of a fiery red skirt grazing her ankles hurried past us, heading for Waverly Place. Asher

Zylberstein regarded her, then sadly shook his head as if he were lamenting his lost youth. "What was I saying?" he inquired.

"You weren't saying anything interesting."

He produced a mordant chortle. "You are a man after my own heart, Mr. Trotsky, frank to a fault. Cards on the table, as the Americans say."

I could feel Litzky's sizzling breath singeing my inner ear. *Be sure to keep your goddamn cards off the goddamn table, Bronshtein.*

"I am, have been for more decades than I care to count, a keen as mustard Zionist," Zylberstein was saying. "Are you familiar with the Zionist movement, my dear Trotsky?"

"I remember my father reading aloud a leaflet he found in our mailbox. It was signed by that Austrian journalist Herzl and described his scheme to convince the Jewish population in the Pale of shtetls to emigrate to Palestine."

"Emigrate to Palestine and recreate a Jewish homeland in biblical Israel."

"My father thought it was a harebrained scheme. I can't say that I disagreed with him then. Or now. If you've come to me because you think, being Jewish, I see Zionism as the solution for Russia's Jews—"

"I have come to you because over time I, too, have come to believe that creating a Jewish homeland in Palestine is, as you so colorfully put it, a harebrained scheme. In an ideal world, the ideal solution would be a Jewish homeland in Palestine.

We have people trying to persuade the British foreign secretary Balfour to publish a formal declaration, something along the lines of Great Britain looking with favor on the establishment of a Jewish homeland in Ottoman Palestine, but even with such a declaration I don't hold out hope that this will happen in my lifetime. Even if the British could somehow be convinced to permit it, please explain to me how a relative handful of Jews would keep their heads above water in a sea of Arabs."

From a pocket of his duffel coat, Zylberstein produced a thin packet wrapped in newsprint and bound in rubber bands and set it on the bench between us. "It's not another pastrami sandwich," he said with a chuckle. "There's one thousand U.S. dollars in fifty-dollar bills in it—this should more than cover your steamship passage back to Russia."

I suppose my confusion registered on my face. "Why?"

"Like me, you're an Israelite, my dear Bronshtein—"

"You know my name?"

"I have friends in Washington who let me see a copy of the Bureau of Investigation's dossier on one Lev Bronshtein, a.k.a. Leon Trotsky. Several of their bureau's informants are convinced you're an anarchist, others suggest you are a Menshevik. Your collaborators at *Novy Mir* appear to be persuaded you have taken up residence in Lenin's camp and identify as a Bolshevik. The one thing they all agree upon is you are Russian, and a steadfast revolutionist."

"What exactly do you want from me, Mr. Zylberstein?"

"I expect you will be joining the other Bolsheviks returning to Petrograd once you are able to cough up the boat fare. Josef Stalin, your Georgian bank robber who has been supplying valises filled with rubles to Mr. Lenin, is thought to be on his way back from a Siberian prison. Your Vladimir Lenin is making plans to cross Germany en route to Petrograd in a sealed railroad wagon; as Lenin proposes to take Russia out of the war, one can reasonably assume the kaiser will be only too happy to waive the train fare and expedite his return."

"Why would an American aluminum magnate who owns a Hudson Super Six and employs a chauffeur to drive it want to finance my return to Russia?"

"It's a long story. Are you sure you want to hear it?"

I swallowed the last of my pastrami. "One thousand U.S. dollars buys my undivided attention."

"Indeed." He collected his thoughts. "Where to start? One of my prized possessions is a Hebrew Bible printed in Vilna in 1879. On the inside of the cover there is a prayer, handwritten by my grandfather. The prayer had Jews beseeching God to watch over the health of the czar, Aleksander Nikolayevich, his wife, Maria Aleksandrovna, and their son, the crown prince Aleksander Aleksandrovich. My grandfather's prayer, my dear Trotsky, went unanswered: Aleksander Nikolayevich, known to the world as Aleksander II, was assassinated two years later. After his assassination, anti-Semitic pogroms exploded in Russia when the *farshtunken* czarists spread revolting rumors that the terrorists responsible were commanded by Jews. Are you familiar with the czar's advisor Konstantin Pobedonostsev? Ah, there's one name that has not gotten stuck on the tip of my tongue! His formula to solve the so-called Jewish problem in Russia was notorious: 'One-third conversion, one-third emigration, one-third starvation.'"

The name Pobedonostsev rang an ominous bell. "When my father came in from our pigsty," I remembered, "he used to wipe his shoes on a homemade doormat with Pobedonostsev's portrait on it."

"Just so. In my dotage I have my own—forgive me if I borrow your expression—harebrained idea: That Mr. Lenin's Bolsheviks—inspired by Karl Marx, the grandson of a rabbi and the descendant of Talmudic scholars; inspired by you, Lev Bronshtein, a nonobservant Jew who also eats kosher; inspired by your Vladimir Lenin himself, who thanks to his maternal great-grandfather is said to have Jewish blood in his Bolshevik veins—that Mr. Lenin's Bolsheviks are the last best hope to do away with anti-Semitism in Russia."

For Pete's sake, Bronshtein, don't look a gift horse in the mouth—take the damn money before he changes his mind.

Litzky was right, of course. I slipped the wad of fifty-dollar bills into the pocket of my sealskin coat. "If we manage to take power in Russia," I said, "we Bolsheviks will establish a dictatorship of the proletariat, and that, Mr. Zylberstein, will in turn asphyxiate anti-Semitism. Once the workers and peasants are freed from the czarist yoke and capitalist exploitation, the anti-Semitism and class distinctions that cripple Russian society will simply cease to exist. The former czar's Kremlin will become the Kaaba of global Communism."

"Brave words, Mr. Trotsky. *HaShem* should only hear them."

"Everybody wins if we give Russian Jews a reason to stay in Russia and not risk emigrating to a sliver of land filled with people who will not welcome them." I looked at my benefactor, at a loss for words. "I'm not sure how to thank you—" I finally managed to blurt out.

"I'm not looking for thanks, dear boy, I'm looking for revolution that will benefit Jews." He hesitated. "You, being Russian, will likely not be familiar with Shakespeare's last play, *Tempest*. In the last speech of the last scene of his last play, Prospero is asked if he thinks about death. 'Every third thought,' he replies. That's where I'm at, my dear Trotsky. You're what—thirty-five?"

"Thirty-eight."

"At thirty-eight, Mr. Trotsky, you are knocking on life's door. I'm an old man knocking on death's door. Doing what I can to promote revolution in Russia to save the Jews is my life's work reduced to one desperate gesture." He stood up. So did I. "I should like to put a personal question to you."

"Put. Put."

"It is generally known, you certainly made no secret of it, that you hoped to trigger a worker's revolution here in the

New World. Giving up on America must surely be a bitter pill for you to swallow."

Tell him about the damn birch trees, Litzky breathed into my inner ear.

I cleared my throat that didn't need clearing, a nervous tic of mine when a conversation stumbles onto the quicksand of intimacy. "On my father's farm in Ukraine," I explained, "I would wake up at sunrise every morning and gaze through the narrow window at the peeling branches of the birch trees to see which way the wind was blowing, and with what force. Here, in New York, I study the grim faces of the workers crowded into the Third Avenue Elevated to see which way the political wind is blowing, and with what force. I come away with the queasy feeling that America is becalmed—there is little appetite for serious change, much less for revolution. The workers and their syndicalists aren't interested in the ultimate solution, owning the means of production, running the factories, sharing the profits—they spend their waking hours fighting for a juicier slice of the capitalist pie. In short, my exhortations to revolution fall on stone-deaf ears. Still—"

"Do go on, Mr. Trotsky. Still?"

"I was going to say that if we Bolsheviks can succeed in rousing Russian workers to revolution, it will inevitably light a fire under the proletariat in Germany, in Austria, in France, in England. And why not here in America? I am convinced that only the triumph of the proletariat in the

West can protect our Russian revolution from a bourgeois counterrevolution."

"Hmmm. Interesting. I have read your book *Results and Prospects*—I recognize your concept of permanent revolution, if I'm not mistaken."

"You are not mistaken."

"Another personal question, Mr. Trotsky, if I may: If for some reason you couldn't be a professional revolutionist, I'm curious to know what would be your second choice."

Curiosity killed the cat, Litzky reminded me. *Though I need to admit it's a titillating question.*

"Like a snake that outgrows one skin and presents itself to the world in a new guise," I said, "I've worn many skins in my life—farmhand on my father's Ukraine acres, Odessa gymnasium student, Marxist union organizer, Siberian jailbird, Balkan war correspondent, anti-Lenin Menshevik, pro-Lenin Bolshevik, to name just a few. Without regret I shed these skins when I felt it was time to move on and become someone else. Looking back, Mr. Zylberstein, I suspect that the skin I was most comfortable in was the one I first wore. You'll laugh, but when I was a teenager on my father's farm, I had a measure of affection for pigs. If I couldn't make revolution, I think I'd be quite content running a swine farm."

"Well, speaking as an occasionally observant Jew who, like you, also eats kosher, I for one am glad you prefer revolution to raising pigs," Zylberstein quipped. He glanced at the watch on his skeletal wrist. "Oh dear, I fear I must be off," he said.

Don't just stand there gaping, Bronshtein. The man's just given you a ticket back to Russia. The very least you can do is shake his damn hand, for Christ's sake.

We shook hands. "Thank you for the overpriced pastrami sandwich," I said.

He laughed. "Half the sandwich was mine."

17

Now that the czar has stopped being czar . . .

SITTING AT OUR MINUSCULE KITCHEN table on Vyse Avenue in the Bronx, with the low-wattage electric bulb dangling from the ceiling turning our skin sallow, I recounted my meeting with this Zylberstein person to Nata in a whisper so as not to wake the boys sleeping in the next room. She shook her head in befuddlement, then removed the rubber bands and, moistening her thumb, carefully counted out the crisp new fifty-dollar bills. I grasped that counting the bills was the one thing that would convince her I wasn't making up the story about the aluminum magnate. "The ship will stop for fuel at Halifax, Nova Scotia—as it's a Royal Navy port and the United Kingdom manages Canada's external affairs, we'll need visas from the British," I said. "I'll tend to that detail tomorrow."

"But will the British give you visas?"

"We are Russian citizens, traveling with valid Russian

passport papers, returning to our homeland. How can they refuse?"

"Even with visas, will they let you continue the voyage?"

"I don't expect the local British authorities in a backwater like Halifax to know who Leon Trotsky is."

Behind us the kitchen door opened very slowly. Our oldest son, Lyova, stood on the threshold, clutching the waistband of his pajamas to keep them from falling around his bare feet. "Can't sleep," he said in a sleepy voice.

Nata filled a glass with water from the faucet and held it out, but he shook his head. "Not thirsty," he told us. "Scared."

"Scared about what?" I asked.

"Sergei and me, we're not stupid—we know, now that the czar has stopped being czar, you're going back to Russia."

"Is that a problem?" I inquired.

"Are you taking us with you?"

Nata burst out laughing. "We are absolutely taking you with us," she exclaimed. "We wouldn't dream of going anywhere without our sons. Where we go, you go too."

Lyova still looked worried. "When we arrived in New York," he said, "you told us we'd be Russian in America. Going to school here in the Bronx all these weeks, America has rubbed off on us. A lot of American words are trapped in my head. Will they let me and Sergei back into Russia if we are a teeny bit American? Will we be American in Russia?"

I hefted my firstborn son up onto my knees. "You will be Russian in Russia, my darling Lyova," I told him. "You will be, like your mother, like me, Russian to the marrow of your eleven-year-old bones no matter where you are."

He seemed relieved. "Does this mean I can skip doing homework?" he asked seriously. "I mean, if I'm not going to be here, how can I hand it in?"

Nata's and my eyes met and we had a hard time keeping our faces straight. "Yes, it's okay, this once, to skip the homework, Lyova," I told him.

18

Trotsky and Lenin are going to repair Russia . . .

AN OVERNIGHT BLIZZARD OF SNOW and sleet that turned to rain in the early hours of the morning had deposited ankle-deep slush on the nearly deserted streets of Manhattan. But neither my waterlogged boots nor the leaks that short-circuited subway stations, stranding passengers, me among them, on badly lit platforms waiting for trains that were running late when they ran at all, could dampen my spirits: The czar was unemployed and the Bronshteins were going home to Mother Russia! In my quest for British visas, I finally made it to the massive high-rise at 44 Whitehall Street in lower Manhattan Island only to discover that the bank of elevators servicing the maze of offices was out of service—a janitor said something about flooding in the basement short-circuiting the lifts. Undaunted, I climbed the nine floors to the British consulate to join the line snaking out the door and down the hallway. I counted noses—I was eighteenth on the line filled with Russians seeking British visas for the pit stop at Halifax in Nova Scotia. "I recognize you," the woman just in front of me said. "You're Leon Trotsky. I heard you speak at the Cooper Union." The woman gestured for me to pass in front of her. "Comrades," she called, "Leon Trotsky is queuing for a British visa."

The word made its way up the line.

"It's the man himself, Leon Trotsky!"

"Trotsky in the flesh!"

"He looks younger than his picture in the newspaper."

"He looks happier than his picture in the newspaper, you ask me."

"Happier than a clam at high tide," a young mother nursing a baby under her shawl agreed.

"Celebrating the end of three centuries of Romanov rule would make any Russian happier," a man wearing a felt Mongolian *loovuuz* on his head said.

"Let Trotsky through, comrades," an old man on crutches cried. "He and Vladimir Lenin are going to repair Russia."

And one by one the Russians queuing for British visas shooed me past until I was inside the consulate's door and next in line at the single desk where visas were issued. "Passports," the clerk wearing a starched wing collar intoned without looking up from his bank of official stamps. He adjusted the eyeglasses on his nose and glanced at the four sheets of official paper I set down on the desk. "Bron-*shtein*, Lev," he said, finally looking up at me as he stressed the last syllable of my family name. "Purpose of your trip to Halifax?"

"My family and I are on our way back to Russia," I said. "The steamship company told me the *Kristianiafjord* had to put in at Halifax to top off its fuel bunkers for the Atlantic crossing. Halifax being a Royal Navy port—"

"The vessel stops at Halifax so our local authorities there can search the passengers for contraband. Will you be shipping contraband back to Russia, Mr."—he looked down at my passport paper—"Mr. Bron-*shtein*?"

"The only things we'll have with us are my Serbian army duffel bag and two valises filled with clothing," I told him.

"No weapons for the insurrection the czar's enemies hope to incite?"

Yo, my man Bronshtein, for once in your life forgo the primeval pleasure of antagonizing a government flunky, Litzky barked into my mind's ear.

But I couldn't resist. "No weapons," I shot back, "unless you consider Marx's *Communist Manifesto* a weapon." And looking my interlocutor dead in the eye I delivered Marx's famous line: "Proletarians have nothing to lose but their chains."

Half a dozen Russians within earshot applauded. My British pen pusher's mouth curled into a sneer. "Where did you get the three hundred twenty dollars for the second-class passage, Mr."—he glanced again at my passport paper—"Bron-*shtein*?"

"I put money aside for a rainy day. In case you haven't noticed, it's raining outside today."

"Wise guy, are we?"

I thought I saw the clerk nod imperceptibly to someone on the catwalk overlooking the hall. I turned to look up—and recognized the gentleman with a short military haircut and long sideburns that curled around his flushed cheeks. My heart sank and I feared the worst: One word from Sir William Wiseman, Britain's intelligence constable in New York, and I'd never set foot on the Norwegian steamship, much less in Petrograd. You can imagine my relief when I saw the clerk exhaling onto his official rubber visa stamp, then thumping it down next to the embossed imperial eagles on each of our four passport papers and inking in the date and his signature.

"Thank you, thank you," I mumbled.

"If it'd been up to me—" He didn't finish the sentence.

My heart, as the saying goes, skipped a beat and I had the nagging sensation that Sideburns didn't wish me Godspeed when he decided to let me leave New York for Nova Scotia. Still, I would soon be on my way back to Mother Russia and this was cause to rejoice. Collecting our passports, I started toward the door, shaking hands with the Russians on the queue who had pushed me to the head of the line. The woman who had first identified me grabbed my elbow as I passed. "Good luck to you, Leon Trotsky," she said. "Russia's history won't be the same if it's written by you and your Bolshevik comrades."

19

I will make my revolution without a conscience . . .

FROM THE MOMENT I FIRST looked into my father's cracked mirror and noticed the shadow of a bristling beard on my sixteen-and-a-half-year-old chin, I have been meticulous about shaving come rain or come shine—it's a daily ritual that soothes my soul as it smooths my chin. Even in the czar's Siberian penal colony, where a bar of soap was a curiosity, I managed to exchange twenty rubles and my two-volume collected works of Pushkin for a straight-edge razor and a small wooden bowl of Chinese shaving cream. But here in New York the excitement of packing up my family and wrangling a visa from the British consulate and arranging for passage back to Russia hadn't left me with time to eat a square meal, much less shave, which accounted for the three-day stubble of a mask on my face. To make matters worse, I hadn't found time to get the haircut I badly needed. Looking more like one of those American hobos marooned between freight trains than an aspiring Russian revolutionist,

I turned up at the titanic Harlem River Casino on 127th Street for the leave-taking bash my young Communist friend Lou Fraina and his comrades had organized. Hundreds of rain-drenched Socialists, stinking of wet wool and camphor, dozens of them dancing Fred's "Turkey Trot" to the music being belted out by a five-man band on the stage, were jammed into the enormous hall decked with giant red banners. "Come meet Emma Goldman, the anarchist who shocked the pants off America with her opinions on free love," Lou shouted over the racket, pulling me toward one of the trestle tables set up under the stage. "She just finished a stretch at the Blackwell's Island jail. Emma, Emma, say hello to Leon Trotsky, the Bolshevik who has high hopes of overthrowing the post-czarist Provisional Government and putting Comrade Lenin in power in Petrograd."

A handsome woman who looked as if she were pushing fifty from the safer side fitted a monocle onto one eye and peered up at me. "With all this racket that they call music, I didn't catch your name," she yelled.

"Trotsky, Leon," I yelled back.

"Ah, our guest of honor! You're esteemed in some circles and notorious in others," she yelled. "You could use a haircut." She waved a hand in the direction of the five-man band belting out noise over our heads. "Being Russian, I don't expect you're familiar with the American author Mark Twain. He is supposed to have suggested that Wagner's music was better than it sounded. Alas, the same cannot be said for these raucous gentlemen."

A group at one end of the vast hall began waving small red flags and singing "The Marseillaise." In an instant hundreds of people were singing along with them, drowning out the "Turkey Trot." "I am only able to identify two tunes," I confided to Miss Goldman. "One is 'The Marseillaise.' The other's not." She rewarded my witticism with a hoot of laughter.

Above us on the stage, the five band members began packing away their instruments. Emma Goldman bounded to her feet and, grabbing hold of my elbow, pulled me closer. "I'm a diehard atheist," she confessed, her face so near mine I got a whiff of something best described as the absence of perfume. "But I hope to God the American workers take their cue from your Russian comrades and send the capitalist sons of bitches packing."

As "The Marseillaise" wound down, Lou scrambled up onto the stage and grabbed hold of the microphone. "Comrades," he cried, his voice booming from loudspeakers around the hall. "We are here tonight to honor the great Russian revolutionist Leon Trotsky, to wish him well as he sails off tomorrow back to his homeland. History is being made. Let's hear it for the man who is making it, L-e-o-n T-r-o-t-s-k-y!"

Wild cheers and foot-stamping echoed from the rafters of the great hall. Emma Goldman pushed me toward the steps leading to the stage. "Light the fire," she shouted into my ear. I clambered onto the stage and peered out at the sea of Socialists' faces, their cheers ringing in my ears. Several times I gestured for quiet but they kept cheering and stamping their feet until Lou stepped up to the microphone. "Comrades, comrades, we need to simmer down and listen to the man," he shouted. Gradually the tumult petered out. I leaned toward the microphone but before I could get a word out it squealed like a cat in heat. The crowd roared with laughter. Lou adjusted the height of the microphone and stepped back. I tried again. "Comrades, Socialists, Communists, workers of the world, vanguard of the proletariat," I began. Scanning the audience I spotted Fred sitting on a trestle table on one side of the hall, her legs crossed at her delicious knees, her short skirt rising on her thighs, and I added, looking directly at her, "precious friends."

The crowd broke into a spontaneous chant: "Trot-sky, Trot-sky, Trot-sky." And I could see Fred mouthing my two-syllable name and applauding happily. I held up the palms of my hand as if I were surrendering to their excitement, which gradually died away to a stifling stillness. You could have heard a pin drop. "When revolution calls," I cried, "revolutionists respond. The world is our country, comrades—we live for it, we fight for it, and if need be we are ready to die for it."

"We're ready to kill for it!" a woman screamed. The crowd cheered.

"Tomorrow morning at a South Brooklyn pier I board the Norwegian steamship that will take me back to Russia to overthrow the Provisional Government and put an end to this ruthless war that pits Russian workers against German workers." Realizing that the hundreds of Socialists present were hanging on my every word, I lowered my voice to a hoarse whisper. "For this so-called world war must be seen for what it really is: A clash of warmongering imperialists, America's Morgans fighting Germany's Bleichröeders fighting France's Rothschilds fighting England's Churchills." I suddenly felt dizzy and gripped the microphone to steady myself. "There is only one war, comrades, and that's the class struggle. There is only one enemy," I plunged on. Intoxicated by my own voice and raising it to a shrill cri de coeur, I spit out the rest of the sentence: "Capitalism!"

A storm of triumphant applause rose toward the ceiling and I had the momentary fantasy that the intensity of the swell would actually lift the roof off the Harlem River Casino.

"You were spellbinding!" Fred exclaimed when I had made my way through the horde, shaking hands left and right, to her trestle table. "You had the crowd eating out of the palm of your perspiring hand. Harlem has never seen anything like you."

"We need to talk," I told her.

"We need to screw," she shot back. "Electricity has to be discharged after a violent lightning storm." She laughed when she saw the expression on my face. "My place or yours?" she demanded.

"Anyplace," I retorted.

"Anyplace" turned out to be the fourth-floor walkup bedsit of a onetime lover of hers in a tumbledown brownstone on 123rd Street just off Second Avenue with, improbably, a stained-glass skylight depicting snakes in the Garden of Eden. "First things first," Fred announced, stripping to the skin and, standing in front of the tiny sink in the corner of the room, washing her genitals. "Your turn," she said, tossing me the bar of soap.

Later, we got around to the conversation I was aching to have with her. "Here's the thing," I began. "I would like you to come back to Russia with me."

I noticed the melancholy grin before she began to gnaw on the inside of her cheek, obviously at a loss for words. "You're married," she finally managed.

"The woman I'm legally married to is in Siberia," I reminded her.

"I didn't mean that woman. You live in the Bronx with your longtime companion. You once told me that her being the mother of your two sons was a stronger bond than marriage. So in my book, you're married to her even if you aren't married to her."

"Natalya knows about you," I said.

"You told her?"

"Not in so many words. But yes, she knows. Look, Fred,

there will be dozens of Communists returning to Russia with us. You would fit in. Join the group boarding the ship tomorrow, come back to Petrograd with me. I'll organize a flat for you, I'll set you up with a job in our Political Bureau, a salary."

"And now and then you'll turn up to fuck with me."

"To be with you. To make love to you. More than now and then."

"You're a queer bird, Leo. Forgetting for a moment that I'm not about to play second fiddle, I don't happen to be a revolutionist." Sitting on the mattress, she tugged the sheet up to her chin. "Tell me something, Leo, what attracts you to me?"

"I see you as a kindred spirit. I like that you're one of a kind, the original model. I like that you're unpredictable—I never know what you're going to say next. I'm never quite sure what you're going to do next."

"A kindred spirit with a female body."

Aiii, she's got you by the balls, Bronshtein.

"Look, I don't deny that I am attracted to your body, Fred. I'd be stone blind if I weren't. But being attracted to the body of a kindred spirit is not a crime. While we're on the subject, what do you see in me?"

"Ha! Your body is reasonable enough, your circumcised dick is exploitable, you are a quick study—you picked up on reciprocity before I could explain it."

"That's it? That's all?"

"The truth is you fascinate me, Leo. I can understand someone who is ready to die for a cause he believes in—I am, after all, my father's daughter."

There's a but *coming, for sure,* Litzky predicted.

"But . . . but I don't understand someone who is ready to kill for a cause." I couldn't miss the tear in her voice as she finished the thought. "My father drew the line at killing for a cause and it cost him his life. I follow in his footfalls. I draw the line where my father drew the line: I admit to carrying a torch for you, Leo, but I don't carry a torch for revolution in Russia. I absolutely refuse to kill for it."

"In Russian we say *Konets—vsemu delu venets*: The end crowns the work. You draw the line because you don't have a cause, something you believe in so deeply that the end justifies any and all means."

"I am wary of causes because they are so easily manipulated by men—always men, never women—for whom the end is usually power or fame or fortune."

"You are a dyed-in-the-wool cynic, my dear Fred."

"And you're not?"

Litzky repeated her question. *And you're not, Bronshtein?*

"Not yet," I said, addressing both Fred and Litzky. "With luck, not ever," I added.

"Well, I dearly hope you somehow manage to survive the revolution you plan to ignite."

"Igniting a revolution is child's play. Surviving the

revolution can be complicated. Listen, what can I say to make you change your mind about coming to Russia with me?"

The tight-lipped grin reappeared on her anxious face. She shook her head ever so slightly. "Nothing."

"Surely there must be—"

She cut me off. "Nothing," she repeated.

Litzky startled me by joining the conversation. *So, Bronshtein: Me, too, I'm not going back with you either and for the same reason as Fred. A conscience worth his salt will draw the line at killing for revolution.*

The grating voice in my mind's ear sent a shudder of alarm down my spine. What h-h-happened to conscience l-l-loyalty? I stammered, my thoughts tripping over each other in my brain. You are not p-p-permitted to abandon m-m-me . . . after all these years.

It's you who's abandoning me, Bronshtein!

Screw you, Litzky. I will make my revolution without a conscience, I told myself.

Fred regarded me curiously, her lips pursed. "Funny thing about you, Leo. This isn't the first time I've had the uncomfortable feeling—it comes from watching your wandering eye lose its focus—that you're having a conversation with someone other than me."

"I often am," I confessed.

"Who are you talking to?" she demanded.

"My conscience."

"I'm relieved to hear you have one. I don't see you organizing a revolution without a conscience."

"Had one. Seems as if I don't have one anymore."

"Oh, my poor orphaned Leo!" Fred cried. "However will you cope without a conscience?"

First thing Tuesday morning, March 27, 1917, ten weeks and two days after I set foot in the New World, I telephoned Henry Feuer at his Bronx furniture shop. "It's me, Leon Trotsky, Mr. Feuer. You need to come collect your furniture. I'm going home today."

20

I have seen the future and it works . . .

IF, AS MY FATHER ONCE cautioned me, arrivals open chapters, departures, haunted as they often are by a shadow of regret, must surely close them.

My pal Lou Fraina arranged for a friend of a friend to ferry us in his olive green Pierce-Arrow to the South Brooklyn dock for the closing of my chapter in New York—the midmorning sailing of the *Kristianiafjord.* It was drizzling and a sea of black umbrellas greeted us as we approached the pier. From a distance it looked like a gathering of mourners at a funeral. Sopping red banners drooped from lampposts and the two smokestacks of the ship that would take us to Norway (we planned to continue on to Petrograd by train) belched black smoke into New York's overcast sky, obscuring Manhattan in the distance. Wet faces appeared under the umbrellas and a damp cheer rose from the pier when the reception committee caught sight of me. In exasperation, I turned up the collar of my sealskin coat against the morning chill and snapped at Lou, who was helping Nata retrieve my duffel and our two valises from the Pierce-Arrow's boot, "Whose brilliant idea was this?"

"Most of the comrades here were at the River Casino last night," Lou said. "They heard you say you were leaving from a South Brooklyn pier." He shrugged. "Not my fault if they want to see Trotsky off." He handed me a brown envelope filled with what the Americans called simoleons. "It's the cash we collected last night when we passed the hat," he explained. "There's three hundred twenty-eight greenbacks in it." I started to refuse but he pushed my hand away. "Spend it on revolution," he said with a laugh.

Before I could argue, several men in blue longshoreman smocks hiked me onto their shoulders and deposited me on an enormous wooden packing case. Thinking I was being kidnapped, Sergei shrieked—until his mother told him the crowd had put his father on the packing case the better to hear him speak. "Favor us with a few parting thoughts," Lou yelled up at me. The journalists in the crowd produced small notebooks from their pockets.

"Let me share an anecdote that explains why masses of women in Petrograd, risking their lives to demonstrate for peace and land and bread, obliged Czar Nicholas to abdicate," I began. "This autocratic ruler, the last of the corrupt Romanov dynasty that dates back to the seventeenth century, turns out to have been not only a blood tyrant but a rude son of a bitch. It is said that he deigned to visit the

Hermitage—the great museum adjoining the Winter Palace that housed the art collection of Catherine the Great—one Sunday when the museum was shut. The director assumed the czar would want a tour of the museum to see the famous paintings. But Nicholas settled his royal rump onto a throne-like chair and commanded that they bring the paintings, one by one, to him. The czar didn't visit the museum, friends, the museum visited the czar! The Greeks have a word for this: *Hubris.* Which is appropriately defined as vanity that goeth before a fall."

I heard a scattering of applause. "Hell of a story," Lou called up to me encouragingly.

"Comrades," I went on, "I am about to embark on the first leg of my journey back to Petrograd to join Vladimir Lenin and our Bolshevik comrades in consigning the Romanovs and the post-czarist Provisional Government to the dustbin of history. We shall, with any luck, put an end to the vicious war that drives Russian workers onto the bayonets of German workers." I lifted a palm to cut off the cheers and raised my voice to a shrill shout. "I have seen the future, comrades, and I am here to tell you that it works!"

"Mr. Trotsky," one of the journalists yelled to get my attention. "Ryback, from the *New York Tribune.* Rumor has it that you were arrested in New York."

"I was never arrested. I was questioned for three long days about what Vladimir Lenin plans to do if and when he takes power in Russia. I let your American Bureau of Investigation in on a state secret: Comrade Lenin's first order of business will involve simplifying the Russian alphabet to make it more accessible for the up-to-now illiterate peasants."

"Povich, the *Evening World*," a lady journalist hollered. "Your ship is scheduled to put in at Halifax, which as you know is a British-controlled port. The London press claims that you are more dangerous to British interests than the kaiser. Do you seriously expect the British authorities to let you continue your voyage back to Russia?"

"I have a valid British visa and a valid Russian passport. They cannot legally detain me."

A familiar face materialized from under one of the black umbrellas in the crowd. With what I can only describe as a shooting pang of regret, I instantly recognized Fred's signature tight-lipped smile. "Fédora, from the *Brooklyn Daily Eagle*, Mr. Trotsky," she called. "In the ten years since you escaped from a Siberian prison, you have lived in exile in London and Vienna and Geneva and Paris and, until today, here in New York. Can you tell us which one of these cities you liked the most?"

I glanced at Nata but she was crouching and talking to the boys, thank goodness. "Each in its own way was unforgettable," I said. "It would be difficult to . . . New York! By all means, New York. I will remember my ten weeks and two days here until my dying day."

I saw Lou Fraina blotting a drop from an eye as he reached to help me climb down from the packing case. "Ah, Lou, *dolgiye provody—lishniye slyozy*: Long farewells, extra tears!"

"It's not a teardrop, Leon. It's a raindrop."

I put a hand on his shoulder. "I stand corrected," I told him.

He nodded and kept nodding, not trusting himself to put his distress into words.

The cheering—along with cries of *do svidaniya* and *auf Wiedersehen* and *au revoir*—was still ringing in my ears as Nata and I and the boys, lugging our baggage, made our way up the gangway to the *Kristianiafjord.*

"Are they cheering because they're glad we're going?" Sergei asked his mother.

"They're cheering because your father is returning to Russia to fix the country," she told him.

A ship's officer with gold braid on his shoulders stamped our passage and a sailor with his hair tied in a pony's-tail knot led us below deck to the second-class cabin the four of us were sharing. We could feel the deck quivering under our feet as the *Kristianiafjord* began to back away from the pier into the East River. I took the boys and Nata up to the second-class lounge on the main deck so we could all watch as the ship slipped past the Statue of Liberty.

"Oh," Sergei cried excitedly, nose pressed to the rain-stained window. "I remember her—it's Lady Liberty!"

"You called her something else," Lyova said. "You called her a horse."

"A Trojan horse," Nata said with a laugh. "Your father thought the French gift to America was a Trojan horse."

"What makes one horse Trojan and another not, Papa?" Lyova asked.

"A Trojan horse is a hollow wooden statue of a horse in which Greek soldiers hid in order to destroy the Trojan city of Troy," I explained.

"Is Lady Liberty hollow too?" Lyova demanded. "Are there French soldiers hiding in it to destroy New York?"

Nata clasped a palm over her mouth to stifle a laugh. "Not that I am aware of," I replied, suppressing a smile.

Once we passed the harbor's Narrows, with Staten Island a smudge on the horizon behind us, the sea turned choppy, filling with whitecaps, and the *Kristianiafjord* began to pitch as it breasted the waves. Icy winds and the salt spray made going on deck impossible so I installed Nata and the boys at a table in the second-class lounge and, dipping into Lou's brown envelope, used one of the dollar bills to pay for glasses of lemonade and sandwiches for Sergei and Lyova, and doughnuts and mugs of coffee for Nata and myself. The waiter spread a white tablecloth and sprinkled water on it before setting our drinks down.

Gripping the stanchions and table edges to steady himself, an older gentleman with impressive whiskers and a neatly trimmed goatee made his way to our table. He coughed into his fist to attract my attention. "I beg your pardon," he said, "but I was under one of those umbrellas on the pier and heard you speak. Do you mind?" Not waiting for an answer, he pulled up a chair. "Permit me to introduce myself. My name is Joseph Lincoln Steffens, Mr. Trotsky. I'm a journalist for the *New York Evening Post*—"

I cut him off. "Sorry, Mr. Steffens, but I am not giving interviews."

He scratched at his whiskers. "Not looking for an interview, Mr. Trotsky. Looking for conversation with the fellow who presided over the first Russian soviet in 1905."

I thought I recognized the gentleman's name: Fred, talking about her late father's fate in Mexico, had given me several articles from the *Evening Post* signed by someone named Steffens. "Didn't I read stories under your byline about that mutinous general Pancho Villa and his revolution in Mexico?"

My interlocutor brightened. "Indeed. I rode with him when his troops crossed the border and raided Columbus, New Mexico, last year."

The ship pitched sharply and the four of us grabbed hold of our drinks. "If you're not looking for an interview, what can I do for you?" I inquired.

"I was particularly struck by your declaration that you've seen the future and it works," he said. "Like you, I'm traveling to Russia—I hope to interview your Vladimir Lenin and report on the revolution he expects to ignite. Having written a great deal about corruption in government, I harbor grave qualms about the effect of power on mere mortals, even on pious Marxists like your Mr. Lenin. It has been my experience that power pollutes, Mr. Trotsky, and any group that achieves power, including Mr. Lenin's Bolsheviks, will likely abuse it."

"Comrade Lenin's Bolsheviks are also my Bolsheviks, Mr. Steffens. Revolution in Russia is in its first and early phase. I intend to be in Petrograd for the second phase that will return power to the people who work in the factories and on the farms."

"Your dictatorship of the proletariat," he observed.

"Precisely," I said.

"Well, I pride myself on being open-minded, ready to believe what my eyes see," he said. "My inclination is to hope you're right, Mr. Trotsky—to hope that the future you claim to have seen really does work. If this turns out to be the case, I shall be the first to say so." And he added with a knowing wink, "In print."

Lyova piped up. "My father is not returning to Russia in a Trojan's horse," he insisted.

"I should think not," Mr. Steffens agreed, clearly impressed. He turned to me. "Out of the mouth of babes!" He rose to his feet and, half bowing to Nata, said, "Break a leg, Mr. Trotsky."

"I beg your pardon!" I blurted out, startled.

He grinned. "That's American for good luck in your

endeavors," he said. And clinging to the edges of tables, Mr. Steffens cautiously made his way back across the pitching deck of the lounge.

The sky grew bleaker and the sea's swells soared higher as the *Kristianiafjord*, shuddering as it lurched into each enormous wall of a wave, crept across a thousand miles of endless ocean toward Halifax. Nata and the boys became seasick and kept to our cabin, two decks down; I came up for a breath of fresh sea air and a sandwich now and then, hoping to meet other Russian nationals returning, like me, to the homeland. But aside from the bearded barman and one or two waiters, the lounge remained empty of humans during the three-day crossing. And except for three Canadian merchant sailors, old salts with sea legs from the look of them who had been rescued off New Jersey when their ship was torpedoed, the second-class dining room was likewise empty, though I did manage to snag sandwiches from the kitchen for my family. You can imagine our relief when, on Friday, March 30, the ship reached Nova Scotia's calmer waters, threading its way past the lighthouse at Peggy's Cove into the channel leading to Halifax Harbour, which turned out to be filled with British and Canadian warships, along with twenty or so merchantmen riding at anchor, waiting to run the gauntlet of German U-boats and deliver weapons and munitions to European ports. The *Kristianiafjord*, too, was riding on the anchor it had dropped in the bay when Nata, breathing deeply through her nostrils because she claimed to actually smell the lush land visible to starboard, joined me on deck. As we watched, a sleek white cutter with a Union Jack flapping from a halyard tied up alongside us and half a dozen British sailors wearing cream-colored leggings and armed with rifles fixed with bayonets, along with a bearded naval officer, the gold buttons glistening on his blue jacket, mounted the gangway onto the main deck. "All passengers are to assemble in the first-class dining hall," one of the sailors called through a megaphone. Nata fetched the boys, as well as our passports and visas, and we joined the hundred or so passengers crowding into the hall. The British officer climbed onto the bandstand at one end of the room and spoke into the microphone. "I am Captain O. M. Makins, chief British naval control officer in Halifax," he announced. He peered out over the heads of the passengers, surveying the room. "Which one of you is Lev Davidovich Bronshtein, also known as Leon Trotsky?"

Nata and I exchanged looks; she was clearly frightened. I raised my hand. Two of his sailors, their rifles hanging from shoulder slings, pushed through the crowd and took hold of my upper arms. Captain Makins joined us. "I have orders to take you and your wife and children ashore," he told me.

"I absolutely refuse to go!" I exclaimed. "I paid for passage on the *Kristianiafjord* to Norway, I am in possession of a proper Russian passport and a visa for Halifax issued by the British authorities in New York."

"Do calm yourself, Mr. Trotsky," Captain Makins said in an ominously quiet snarl. "This is surely an administrative hiccup. Once we are able to verify your documents, I expect things will work out to your satisfaction."

I am afraid I must have raised my voice. "Russia is allied with Great Britain in the war," I shouted. "You're treating a Russian passenger outrageously. I refuse to leave the ship."

Captain Makins gestured with a toss of his head. The two sailors started to pull me toward the other British sailors who were blocking the doorway. We passed the American journalist Steffens and I could tell from the way he looked at me that he was alarmed. "Shame on the British," he cried. "You are dishonoring king and country."

"You have your story, Mr. Steffens," I said. "Trotsky arrested by the British in Halifax, Nova Scotia. Please make sure it appears in your *New York Evening Post*." I managed a feeble smile. "We Russians have a saying for situations like this," I called over my shoulder. "*Kaby znal, gde upast', tak solomki by podstelil.*" And I translated the phrase for him: "If I knew where I would fall, I would spread straws there."

Nata and my boys, escorted by several armed sailors, joined me on the main deck near the gangway. Seeing the sailors with their rifles at the ready towering over my sons, a nagging dread suddenly infected my brain: I was convinced they were going to take me ashore and shoot me. I stopped walking but the two sailors gripping my arms pulled me along, my feet dragging on the deck. Seeing this, Lyova leaped ahead of his mother. "Shall I hit them, Papa?" he cried, and I could see the tears brimming in his eyes, I could hear those same tears in his terrified voice.

"Don't hit them," I instructed Lyova. "You risk to hurt them."

Behind us, the thirty or so Russian passengers who, like me, were heading home crowded onto the main deck. Captain Makins turned back, his hand resting on the butt of the large naval pistol in his holster. "If you interfere with a British control officer," he yelled, "you too will be removed from the ship."

A Russian woman with long grey hair defied Captain Makins. "Trotsky is the apostle of liberty," she shouted. "Long live the Socialist revolution."

"England is the enemy of liberty," I cried. "Long live Socialism."

"Shut your fuckin' trap," one of the sailors dragging me toward the gangway ordered, "or we'll shut it for you."

"Should I wash his mouth out with soap, Papa?" Lyova cried. And he burst into terrified sobs.

We ended up spending the night on cots in a dank room in Fort George, the star-shaped fortress on a hill overlooking Halifax, with iron bars on the single window—presumably so no one could leap to his death. Two German prisoners of war wearing frayed naval uniforms brought us tin trays filled with hash and a hodgepodge of overcooked vegetables, most of which were still on the trays when they came back to collect them. The boys eventually fell into a restless sleep, Nata dozed fitfully, I lay there for the interminable hours until dawn with my eyes wide open.

"What shall become of us?" Nata whispered when the first faint suggestion of daylight filtered through the streaked window.

I knelt next to her cot so that our heads were almost touching. "If we are separated," I told her, "you must find a way to send telegrams to the Russian consulate in New York and the Russian embassy in Ottawa. With any luck the New York newspapers will pick up that American journalist's story in the *Evening Post*. Our only hope is to light a fire under the British authorities here. Please repeat after me, Nata: Trotsky, who is in possession of a legal passport and a legal visa and a paid steamship ticket, has been denied his legal rights."

"Trotsky, who is in possession of a legal passport—"

"And a legal visa."

"And a legal visa, as well as a paid steamship ticket, has been denied his legal rights."

"Tell them Trotsky demands their immediate intervention to protect the interests of Russian citizens and the dignity of the government they represent."

"Immediate intervention . . . protect the interests of Russian citizens . . . dignity of the government they represent,"

Nata repeated. She couldn't resist adding: "I'm very frightened, my dear Lev. For you. For the boys."

I retrieved Lou Fraina's envelope filled with cash that I'd stashed in one of my knee socks and slipped it under the coat that Nata had rolled up and used as a pillow. "*Pridyot solnyshko i k nashem okoshechkam*," I whispered. "The sun will come to our windows, I promise you."

With the sun still below the horizon and not yet visible in our single window, four British seamen escorted me down several flights of stairs to an underground garage filled with brown military vehicles. A shiny black Vauxhall—I remembered riding in one like it when I first met Lenin in London in what now seemed like a previous incarnation—was parked in front of the double wooden doors, its motor running, a civilian sitting in the passenger seat next to the civilian driver. A young Canadian naval officer in the back seat pushed the Vauxhall's door open and smiled pleasantly. "Be so kind as to get in, Mr. Trotsky."

I didn't think I had a choice. "Where are you taking me?" I demanded, settling down next to him. The Canadian officer rapped his knuckles on the glass partition separating us from the two civilians in the front. Shifting the car into gear as the double door swung open, the driver edged the Vauxhall up a long ramp and onto a two-lane highway. A second Vauxhall filled with sailors fell in behind us.

"To respond to your question—and surely your fears: I have orders to deliver you to the town of Amherst, roughly an hour and a half down the road from here." He gestured to the lunch box and the thermos flask on the seat between us. "I took the liberty of bringing sandwiches and hot coffee."

"Why Amherst?" I asked. "What's in Amherst?"

He laughed under his breath. "A Canadian prisoner of war facility for German soldiers captured on the Western Front."

"So I am to be a prisoner of war despite being a national of a country allied with Great Britain?"

The Canadian officer shrugged. "I merely follow orders," he said. In an undertone, he added, "Albeit unenthusiastically. My name is Blake, Mr. Trotsky, William Blake, like the famous English poet. I was a lawyer in civilian life. When I was conscripted, the army assigned me to the Canadian Military Justice branch. What will intrigue you—what will explain my lack of enthusiasm for this mission to Amherst—is that I happen to be a card-carrying Socialist, so I not only know who Trotsky is, but I have a great deal of admiration for what you have accomplished, not to mention what you have written."

Hearing this, I breathed a bit easier—I was not being taken out to a remote field and shot. "I wouldn't mind a cup of your hot coffee," I admitted.

Sipping the coffee he had poured from the thermos, I asked him if my wife and children had also been arrested. "Certainly not," he told me. "They are being put up in a lodging house near the Halifax waterfront for the duration."

"The duration of what?"

Blake snickered pleasantly. "For the duration of your tribulations, Mr. Trotsky."

I decided to push my luck with this card-carrying Socialist. "Do you have an idea on what grounds I am being detained?"

"I saw the paperwork," Blake told me. He lowered his voice. "Please give me your word you won't tell anyone you heard this from me—"

"My lips are sealed."

"The coded cablegram was signed by a chap in New York name of Wiseman; I gather he is some sort of big cheese with British intelligence in America. He was giving instructions to his counterpart here in Halifax. This Wiseman fellow seemed to think you had secured funds from Jews and possibly even Germans, that you were returning to Petrograd to join your Vladimir Lenin in overthrowing the post-czarist Provisional Government, that the two of you made no secret of your intention to take Russia out of the war, which, as any idiot could see, would be a disaster for the British and their French allies: Germany, no longer battling millions of Russian soldiers in the east, would be able to concentrate its armies in the west. Wiseman insisted you were more dangerous to British interests than Kaiser Wilhelm himself and ordered the British naval control officer in Halifax, one Captain Makins, to board the *Kristianiafjord* and detain the troublemaker—his words, not mine—named Leon Trotsky. It was imperative, he wrote, that you must not be permitted to continue your voyage back to Russia. Hence your tribulations in Halifax."

The Vauxhall stopped for a red light. The car filled with sailors pulled up behind us. Once the light turned green, we sped past a sprawling shantytown of shacks made of rusting corrugated metal sheets.

"Capitalist prosperity!" I remarked ironically.

"Capitalist paradise lost," William Blake agreed. "It's why I identify as a Socialist."

I turned to him. "I don't suppose there's any way—"

He didn't let me finish the thought. "I have already taken a big risk telling you about Wiseman's paperwork, Mr. Trotsky. Please understand: More I cannot do."

I looked William Blake in the eye. "Speaking as a delegate to the Second Communist International and its thousands of comrades hoping to tear down shantytowns and build rock-solid brick houses for the workers and peasants, I thank you for your solidarity."

William Blake glanced nervously at the two civilians laughing at a joke we couldn't hear thanks to the glass partition. "Every Socialist must contribute his fistful of sand if we have any hope of making a mountain out of a molehill," he confided in a whisper.

"Amen," I said.

21

The ends—a worker's utopia—justifies any and all means . . .

THE SO-CALLED *FACILITY* AT AMHERST turned out to be a makeshift Canadian prison in an abandoned iron factory several soccer fields long and jam-packed with a forest of triple-decker bunkbeds as far as the eye could see. The colossal barracks had been equipped with just four latrines for the eight hundred or so prisoners—not surprisingly there was a queue in front of the toilets twenty-four hours a day. On arriving in Amherst I was escorted to the facility's infirmary, obliged to strip to the skin in front of half a dozen Canadian orderlies and subjected to a humiliating body search. The doctor who filled in what he called my rap sheet meticulously recorded my height (five foot eight and a half inches) and weight (137 pounds), along with the color of my eyes (pale blue) and hair (brown). I was then photographed and fingerprinted. As I was older than most of the German prisoners, I was assigned one of the lowest bunks in the belief that, at thirty-eight, I was too decrepit to scramble into an upper bunk. A Canadian commissary sergeant who looked as if he had a ramrod for a backbone issued me two pairs of laundered German army fatigues and assigned me menial chores—in the weeks that followed I peeled potatoes, I scrubbed toilet bowls, I mopped latrine floors, I lugged garbage cans into an alleyway and spilled their contents into dump trucks. Once my disagreeable chores were done for the day, I took to my bunk and slogged through a two-volume edition of Goethe, which I managed to liberate from a closet filled with used books, to bone up on my German. As spoken German was already on the tip of my tongue from my time in Berlin, I was able to chat up my fellow prisoners, who were curious to discover how a Russian had wound up in a German prisoner of war camp. Sitting on the edge of my bunk in the evenings after mess call, I began to give informal lectures—at first to just a handful of prisoners who, bored to death with interminable card games and having nothing better to do, drifted over to listen. But word quickly spread and I soon had a standing-room-only crowd—including two or three Canadian guards who spoke fluent German—come to hear me explain Marx's dialectic or his theory of surplus value. I eventually became friendly with a group of Bavarian prisoners who, it turned out, had been rescued in 1914 after the Royal Navy sank the imperial German armored cruiser *Sharnhorst.* Whispering in the pitch dark after lights-out, they recounted the last moments of the *Sharnhorst* as it plunged, stern first, into the sea off the Falklands. The young Bavarians made no bones about how much they despised their own government for leading Germany into a two-front war it couldn't win. Taking my cue from my newfound friends, I abandoned the subject of Marxist theory and began lecturing about the revolution that Lenin would surely ignite in Russia. My subject must have struck a nerve. Responding to questions, I expressed the hope that Lenin's revolution in Russia would inspire sister revolutions in other industrialized countries, Germany foremost among them, where an exploited proletariat existed. "When this brutal war finally ends," I remember telling my Bavarian friends at one of these impromptu lectures, "those who survive will have an obligation toward those who went down with the *Sharnhorst*: You must follow the example of our Russian comrades who sacked their czar and get rid of your kaiser, along with the rabid capitalists around him who started this senseless war. You must fashion a worker's utopia in Germany, friends."

"What do we do about the workers who aren't attracted to our utopia?" a bearded Bavarian demanded.

"You need to deal with them the way you deal with gangrene: Purge them without pity."

"It's one thing to eliminate class enemies," a young sailor with burn scars on a side of his face declared. "To be honest, I couldn't in good conscience treat my fellow workers the same way I treat the capitalists who own the factories."

"Hamlet," I said, "famously told us that conscience makes

cowards of us all. If your conscience is standing in the way of revolution and the creation of a worker's utopia, then this impediment, this conscience, must become the first casualty of the revolution."

The disfigured sailor angled his head inquisitively. "You're telling us we need to start our revolution without benefit of a conscience?"

"I'm saying that the ends—a classless, crimeless worker's utopia—justifies any and all means. If your conscience is obstructing these ends, it must be consigned to the dustbin of history."

My exhorting the prisoners to revolution must have been reported to the authorities by one of the German-speaking guards because the very next morning I was waylaid while wrestling with garbage cans in the alleyway and quick-marched, sandwiched between two armed Canadian soldiers, to the office of the camp commandant. The wooden plaque on the table that served as a desk identified him as Colonel Arthur Henry Morris. "I am told you speak English as well as you speak German," he growled, eyeing me with the disdain British officers usually reserve for draft dodgers. He twisted one end of a whisker into a fine point with his fingertips. "What's this I hear about your preaching the virtues of revolution to my German prisoners of war?"

"I was suggesting revolution in Germany—" I started to say but he waved away my words with a flick of a delicate wrist. "Revolutions are notoriously contagious," he blurted, and I could see his face twitching with anger at each sentence. Colonel Arthur Henry Morris was not accustomed to being contradicted. "I have dealt with your kind before," he warned, "whilst posted to India. If you Russians decide to get rid of your czar—"

"We already have," I noted.

"Kindly abstain from interrupting. If, as I was saying, you Russians get rid of your czar and the Germans were to throw out their kaiser, our dear King George—who happens, through no fault of his, to be the kaiser's cousin—will be next on the list. Your kind draw the wrong conclusions when we British, abiding by the letter of internationally recognized legal principles, treat prisoners decently. You take our decency as a sign of weakness. Let me disabuse you, Trotsky: We have protocols for troublemakers like you. Revolution indeed!"

"If, as you say, you are influenced by international legal principles, perhaps you can tell me the basis for my arrest and incarceration."

If anything the colonel's cheeks grew ruddier. "You represent a danger to the present British government—"

"If I represent a danger to the British government, why did this same government issue me a visa for Halifax?"

"You are dangerous to the allies in general. The allies didn't issue you a visa for Halifax."

I could see that this colonial colonel and I were going round in circles. "Can I at least telephone my wife?" I asked.

"Not permitted."

"So much for British decency," I muttered.

"I will however allow you to send her a telegram. Telegrams," he added, "are permitted."

I grasped at the straw. "If telegrams are permitted, I want to send one to the Russian consulate in Montreal."

The colonel considered this. "As you are a Russian national," he said, "I don't see how I can legitimately refuse."

Arthur Henry Morris's aide-de-camp, a baby-faced lieutenant with windowpane-thick eyeglasses, brought me a pad of blank telegrams and a fountain pen. Leaning over the colonel's table, I wrote: "April 5, 1917: Detained by British military authorities without cause stop interned Amherst with German prisoners of war stop demand your immediate intervention to protect interests of Russian citizens and dignity of government you represent."

Absently twisting the other end of his mustache into a fine point, the colonel glanced at the telegram. "You are a rum bird, Trotsky," he said. "It may interest you to learn that my German prisoners are circulating a petition urging us to liberate you. If it were up to me, I'd send you packing forthwith. Can't have our illustrious Russian revolutionist contaminating my German prisoners, can we?"

"Contaminating?"

The colonel was losing patience with me. "Converting them to Communism, what?"

"Communism, Colonel Morris, is the cure, not the disease."

The colonel wagged a finger at his aide-de-camp. "Remove him from my sight before I forget I am an officer and a gentleman," he ordered.

The lieutenant snapped his heels together. "Sir!" he barked and stepping back, he hauled the door of the office open for me.

22

I was finally on my way back to the turbulent future . . .

I WAS JUST SETTLING INTO my bunk with the two-volume Goethe for company late one afternoon, a month into my Amherst ordeal, when an overweight British sergeant major turned up at the door nearest my end of the barrack. "Trotsky, Leon, on the double," he bellowed. "Bring your gear if you have gear." I presumed I was being transferred to another wing of the vast ironwork to prevent me from *contaminating* my Bavarian friends. Tumbling out of the bunk, I stuffed Goethe, along with my civilian clothing and the second pair of army fatigues and my toilet articles, into a cloth laundry sack and presented myself to the sergeant at the door. "Trotsky, Leon, reporting for additional tribulation," I announced, clicking my heels together. Over his shoulder I spotted the shiny black Vauxhall parked near one of the dump trucks in the alleyway, exhaust streaming from its tailpipe, my card-carrying Socialist pal William Blake holding open the back door and waving to me. In the barrack behind me there was a hue and cry from the Bavarians. "They're freeing Trotsky, comrades," someone shouted. In the bat of an eyelash the German prisoners had spilled into the alleyway and formed an honor guard from the door to the Vauxhall. Giddy at the thought that my tribulations might finally be behind me, I made my way past the Bavarians, who stood to attention and saluted.

"One hell of a send-off they're giving you," Blake said as I stashed my laundry sack in the boot and slid onto the back seat. "What did you do to earn it?"

"I incited them to sack their kaiser and organize revolution in Germany when the war was over."

"Crikey, I wondered why they decided to free you. That explains it: Our British monarchy doesn't look on revolution—anywhere, for whatever reason—with a benevolent eye." Blake rapped his knuckles on the glass partition and the Vauxhall headed down the alleyway. Behind us, the Bavarians could be heard chanting "*Langes leben für Trotzki, langes leben für Trotzki.*" Blake twisted in his seat to peer through the rear window. "What are the buggers saying?" he asked.

"They're wishing me the single thing I'm most likely not to have," I said.

"Which is?"

"Longevity."

Blake looked at me sharply. "I didn't take you for a pessimist, Mr. Trotsky."

I snorted. "If anything, I'm a fatalist," I corrected him. "A friend of mine in New York reminded me that revolutions devour their children, which, as we unfortunately know, is historically accurate." I lowered my voice. "What's the real reason they let me out of this *facility* of yours?"

Blake inched closer and, leaning toward me, spoke the words I'd almost given up hope of hearing. "With newspapers in New York and Petrograd running front-page stories about the famous Trotsky being interned with German prisoners of war, not to mention the deluge of telegrams your Natalya and you dispatched like confetti, you upped the ante. The Russian charge d'affaires in London, clearly feeling the pressure, reminded the British Foreign Office that you carried a valid Russian passport. The British Foreign Office reminded the British naval control officer in Halifax who, in turn, ordered the colonel in charge of the Amherst facility to permit the Russian socialist Trotsky to continue on his journey to Russia."

I had to laugh. "*Facility* is your euphemism, my friend, not mine."

William Blake smiled. "*Mea maxima culpa*," he said in an undertone.

Blake delivered me to the lodging house overlooking the Halifax port. Nata and the boys, not having been forewarned, couldn't believe their eyes when an unshaven stranger wearing German army fatigues turned up on their doorstep. Lyova was the first to recognize me. "It's Papa!" he cried as he leaped into my outstretched arms. "Welcome back to civilization, my darling Lev," Nata murmured, running her fingers over the stubble on my chin as she and Sergei hugged me.

I'm not ashamed to say that the four of us celebrated that night in a waterfront bistro with mugs of tap beer for the grown-ups and tall glasses of Canadian apple cider for the boys. At first light the next morning, the thirtieth of April 1917, a harbor scow ferried us out to the Scandinavian American ship *Hellig Olav*, which winched in its anchor as soon as we were safely on board and steamed out of Halifax Harbour, plunging into the sea swells off Nova Scotia on a course that would deliver us to the port city Kristiania in Norway; that would deliver me, after another trek by train, to the mayhem of revolutionary Petrograd.

Ten years after escaping from Russia and six weeks after quitting New York, I was finally on my way back to the turbulent future, hoping against hope that my Bolshevik comrades and I could make it work.

Afterword, in which I recount the fate of Trotsky and his family, as well as several of the historical personages portrayed in the novel...

LEV DAVIDOVICH BRONSHTEIN, A.K.A. LEON Trotsky, made his way back to Russia to organize and direct the 1917 Bolshevik Revolution that Vladimir Lenin instigated. He went on to negotiate the 1918 Brest-Litovsk peace treaty with Germany that ceded a vast chunk of Russian territory to the invaders but ended Russia's participation in World War I. He created and commanded the Red Army that successfully defended the Bolshevik Revolution in the Civil War (1918–1922) waged by the counterrevolutionary White Armies and their anti-Bolshevik interventionist allies (England, France, Czechoslovakia, Japan, the United States) hoping to restore the Romanovs to power. In the course of the brutal Civil War, Trotsky—commanding without benefit of a conscience!—became infamous for arriving at the front in his armored train, lining up the survivors of a Red Brigade that had broken and run before a White assault, ordering every tenth soldier to take one step forward—and then having them shot. As the Civil War raged, Trotsky turned out to be an enthusiastic advocate of Lenin's Red Terror; inspired by the French Revolution's ruthless Reign of Terror that "shortened by a head" the enemies of France's newly created First Republic, the Bolsheviks summarily executed tens of thousands of actual or potential political opponents in an effort to stifle dissent.

Trotsky was widely considered to be the obvious heir and successor to Lenin. But in the early 1920s Iosif Vissarionovich Dzhugashvili, a.k.a. Stalin, named by Lenin to the post of general secretary of the Soviet Union's Communist Party, was dealing with the daily drudgery that the intellectuals had no patience for: Recruiting, organizing and running the party at the regional and local level. Like Bukharin and the other intellectuals in Lenin's inner circle, Trotsky utterly underestimated Stalin; the Gori bank robber who spoke Russian with a Georgian accent turned out to be a diabolical politician. By the time Lenin died, in 1924, it was Stalin, ruling with an iron fist, who controlled the party and the levers of state power, governing the country with the complicity of the All-Russian Extraordinary Commission for Combating Counter-Revolution and Sabotage, the secret police better known by its abbreviated name, Cheka. As the character Fred predicts in *Bronshtein in the Bronx*, under Stalin the dictatorship *of* the proletariat wound up being a dictatorship *over* the proletariat.

Stalin made sure that his archrival Trotsky wasn't even

invited to Lenin's funeral and, in the years that followed, progressively sidelined him from the Politburo, the Central Committee, the Communist Party, and his role commanding the Red Army. The *vozhd'* (tribal chief, supreme leader) eventually forced Trotsky into exile in Alma-Ata and, in 1929, expelled him from Russia altogether. But he couldn't silence him: In book after book, Trotsky attacked his nemesis Stalin, accusing him of exaggerating his role in the Bolshevik Revolution; of being a mass murderer responsible for the death of millions of Ukrainians and Russians; of crippling the Red Army with purges and failing to prepare the country for the inevitable war against Hitler. In *The Revolution Betrayed*, Trotsky didn't mince words: Stalin's Soviet Union was ruled by "greedy, lying and cynical rulers... [who would] devour the workers' state."

In 1937, after wandering for years in Turkey, France and Norway, Trotsky and his companion, Natalya Sedova, found refuge in Mexico, where they were welcomed by two distinguished Communist artists: Diego Rivera and his ravishing wife, Frida Kahlo. (Trotsky had a short but intense love affair with Frida, which inspired me to fantasize about his liaison in New York with Fred, the half-Mexican journalist for the *Brooklyn Daily Eagle*.)

Stalin's bloodlust wasn't sated with merely exiling his outspoken rival. Trotsky's daughter, Nina, twenty-six years old and denied medical care for tuberculosis, died in Moscow in 1928. Her older sister, Zina, an ardent Marxist, wound up in Berlin when her Soviet citizenship was revoked. Suffering from pulmonary tuberculosis, unable to cope with a profound depression after Stalin let it be known that none of the Trotskys in exile could ever return to the Soviet Union, she turned on the stove's gas jets and committed suicide in 1933. She was thirty-two years old.

The husbands of Trotsky's two daughters were executed. Trotsky's older brother, Aleksander, was arrested and shot in 1938, and his younger sister, Olga (the wife of the prominent Bolshevik Lev Kamenev, who was sentenced to death in a 1936 show trial and executed by firing squad), suffered the same fate in 1941.

Aleksandra Sokolovskaya Bronshtein, Trotsky's lawfully wedded wife whom he abandoned in Siberia when he fled a lifelong prison sentence, vanished in the mid-1930s during one of Stalin's Great Purges and was thought to have been executed in 1938.

Trotsky's youngest son, Sergei, returned to Russia with his parents in 1917 but made the fatal mistake of staying in Russia when his father was forced into exile. Arrested and sent to a labor camp, he was shot in 1937. He was twenty-nine years old.

Trotsky's oldest son, Lyova, a passionate disciple of his father and one of his closest collaborators, wound up in a Paris hospital in 1938 for an emergency appendectomy. He was operated on by Russian émigré doctors thought to have ties to the Soviet secret police. After the operation his health quickly deteriorated and, one week shy of his thirty-second birthday, he breathed his last. Trotsky himself was convinced his son had been murdered.

Trotsky, having outlived his four children and knowing Stalin would try to have him assassinated, took refuge in a fortress-like house in Mexico City protected around the clock by armed guards. In 1940 Stalin's secret police managed to infiltrate a Spanish Communist named Ramón Mercader, who was dating Trotsky's secretary, into Trotsky's inner circle. Mercader turned up one hot summer day wearing a raincoat to conceal the ice axe he was smuggling into the fortress. Alone with Trotsky in his study, he planted the axe in his skull. Natalya Sedova, in the next room, heard a shriek of agony. "Lev Davidovich appeared, leaning against the door frame," she remembered. "His face was covered with blood, his arms hung limply by his side." Devoured by the revolution he ignited, the world-infamous revolutionist who claimed to have seen the future and was convinced he could make it work, died in hospital the next day.

Natalya, who met Trotsky in 1902 and never left his side after that, remained devoted to the father of her two sons even when she discovered his affair with Frida Kahlo. She lived in Mexico after his assassination and co-authored a biography of Trotsky. She died in France in 1962 at the age of eighty.

* * *

Nikolai Bukharin: Returning to Russia in 1917, he quickly rose in the Bolshevik ranks to become the party's leading Marxist theoretician. He gained a reputation as a humanist when he took the poets Osip Mandelstam and Boris Pasternak under his wing. In the subsequent power struggle between Stalin and the Old Bolsheviks, Bukharin for a time cautiously sided with Stalin. But he eventually broke with the *vozhd*, opposing Stalin's forced collectivization of agriculture and the liquidation of kulaks who opposed it. In the end Bukharin too was ultimately outmaneuvered and devoured by the revolution he helped make: In 1938 he was arrested, tried for treason and forced to publicly admit to a nonexistent conspiracy of "wreckers." Sentenced to death, he was taken down to the basement of Moscow's Lubyanka prison and executed with a bullet shot into the nape of his neck.

Aleksandra Kollontai: The daughter of an Imperial Russian Army general and a Finnish woman with peasant roots, Kollontai from an early age was a militant Marxist and fervent Communist who passionately promoted the nascent feminist movement and revolution in Russia. She and Trotsky first crossed paths in Saint Petersburg in 1905 when she witnessed the brutal massacre of Russians demonstrating in front of the czar's Winter Palace that became known as Bloody Sunday. When the Bolsheviks seized power in 1917, she was one of the founders of Zhenotdel, the women's department of the Central Committee dedicated to familiarizing females with the revolution's pioneering marriage, education and work laws. She became the first woman to be appointed people's commissar (the equivalent of minister) in the Soviet government, and later was named as the Soviet Union's first female ambassador. She eventually lived abroad for more than twenty years and was careful to keep a low profile, which surely accounted for her being one of a handful of Old Bolsheviks not devoured by the revolution she helped make. She died in Moscow in 1952 at the age of seventy-nine.

Lou Fraina: An ardent and committed Communist and leading theoretician of the American Communist movement, Fraina in 1919 was one of the original founders of the American Communist Party. He edited two of the earliest Communist newspapers in the United States: *The New International* and *The Revolutionary Age.* Targeted by Senator Joseph McCarthy's notorious investigations into Communist influence in America, Fraina was obliged to wage an expensive legal battle to keep from being deported. The action against him was only abandoned when Fraina died of a cerebral hemorrhage in 1953 at the age of sixty-one.